MOVIN' DIFFERENT 2
A HOOD MILLIONAIRE ROMANCE

KEVINA HOPKINS

Movin' Different 2: A Hood Millionaire Romance

Copyright © 2022 by Kevina Hopkins

All rights reserved.

Published in the United States of America.

Published by Cole Hart Signature, LLC.

Mailing List

To stay up to date on new releases, plus get information on contests, sneak peeks, and more,

Go To The Website Below...

www.colehartsignature.com

PREVIOUSLY ON MOVIN' DIFFERENT...

I walked over to the table and sat down. There was baked chicken, rice pilaf, green beans, and dinner rolls. The food looked good, and I was ready to dig in. We all made our plates before Juliet started talking.

"Chase told me you had a doctor's appointment today. What are you having?"

"A boy and a girl." I smiled. In the beginning, I almost went crazy when I found out I was having twins. I had no idea what the hell I was going to do with one kid let alone two. Now I can't wait to meet my bundle of joys. I love them more than anything already and they're not even here yet.

"Okay, how far along are you?"

"I'm seven months."

"How sure are you that that's my son's kids? Are you willing to get a DNA test?"

"Excuse me? I'm not getting a DNA test done. I know who I was sleeping with." Chase's mother had caught me off guard with her question. I couldn't believe she was indicating I was a hoe or something.

"Ma, chill, I don't need a DNA test done. She got pregnant while we were together."

"No, Chase, I'm just trying to be practical about this situation. She disappears for months and then all of sudden she comes back telling you that she's pregnant and it's yours? If she knew she was pregnant by you, why didn't she reach out when she first found out?"

"You don't have to ask him questions about me like I'm not sitting here. I knew he was my kids' father from the beginning, but I wanted a stress-free pregnancy for as long as I could have one."

"Well, you should have thought about that before you got pregnant by a man with a girlfriend. What did you expect to accomplish by keeping these kids? What do you want from my son? You need money or a house, tell me, what is it? I know it can't be a relationship because he's already in one and she's my future daughter-in-law. I will never see you as that. I could never respect someone like you."

"Ma, that's enough. You are out of line," Chase yelled.

"No, let her finish. Let her get it all out her system now because I guarantee you this is the first and last time she will ever get to disrespect me in my face," I fumed.

"What is that supposed to mean?" Juliet challenged me.

"It means exactly what I said. I respect my elders and out of respect for you being Chase's mother, I'm going to say this in the nicest way possible. I'm not sure how much you know or what you know about me, but I don't need Chase and I damn sure don't need you in my or my kids' life. I don't need a house from Chase because I already have one and even if I didn't have one here, I have a place in Miami to live. I'm not some hood booger that's out here broke with no guidance or parents. I am well loved by both of my parents and the rest of my family. I only came back and told Chase about my kids as a courtesy. I told him that he didn't have to be in my kids' life because they'd be good regardless. Let's be real, look at me, I can guarantee you that it won't be hard for me to get my kids a stepdaddy."

"Wait, what the fuck do you mean you can find my kids a stepdad? I'm the only daddy they will ever have. I'll knock you and that nigga wig back," Chase threatened, interrupting me.

I ignored him and put my hands up to stop him from talking while I continued my rant with his mother.

"You ask why I chose to continue this pregnancy even though I knew Chase had a girlfriend? Him having a girlfriend doesn't have shit to do with me or my kids. I don't want Chase anymore but let's be clear, if I wanted him, your future daughter-in-law would be a distant memory. Just know he's only still with her because I don't want him. I already told him that I'll never start a relationship with him again, so I don't ever plan on being your daughter-in-law anyway. I didn't fall for and get pregnant by another woman's man. I fell in love and got pregnant by my man. The man that I thought I would have a future with. It's not my fault that you raised a lying cheater. You were around me and, in my face, knowing he had a girlfriend and not one time did you say anything to me about it. Instead, you plastered a fake smile on your face. Where was this loyalty for your future daughter-in-law then? That says more about you than it does about me," I snapped.

"Listen, little girl, I don't know who you think you're talking to—" Juliet started, but I cut her off.

"No, you listen, as far as I'm concerned, we don't have anything else to talk about. I came so we can have a civilized conversation about my plans with the twins. I didn't have to sit down and talk to you about anything. Chase is the only one that needs to know what's going on with me. You don't have to like me, but you will respect me if you want to be in your grandkids' life."

"You can't stop me from seeing them if they're my son's kids."

"Call my bluff and disrespect me again. At the end of the day, I am their mother and I will have the say in who they can and can't be around."

"Okay, just answer this then. Do you plan on letting my son get his kids on his own? What is he supposed to tell his girl-friend about them? If he stops sleeping with you, are you going to try and keep the kids away from him?"

I couldn't help but chuckle at the audacity of her stream of questioning. As if it was my responsibility to shield his girl-friend and her feelings.

"What he tells his girlfriend is not my concern. It's not my job to care about her feelings. Chase is the one committed to her. When my kids are a bit older, yes, they can go with Chase but until then, no, they will not be going with him. He can come to my house to see them, or I can bring them out here to let him spend time with them. As far as me sleeping with him, that's none of your business. I would never stop him from seeing them unless he's a danger to their well-being."

"Ma, if I knew you were going to act like this, I never would have told McKenzie to come to dinner with you. Half of the questions you're asking her you already know the answers to because I told you. You can't fault her for what's going on. I'm the one you should be mad at. I'm the one that fucked up, but I can't tell you what you want to hear or what Diane will want to hear. I went about things wrong when I got with McKenzie, but I won't call her or my kids a mistake. I will be there for my kids regardless of what you or Diane have to say. If she can't forgive me, then so be it. I'll be moving back out here and making some changes in my life."

"I'm sorry, but I hold both of you accountable for what's going on. Diane just lost your second child last month and now you're about to throw it in her face that you got two kids on the way by somebody else? That will break her, Chase. You need to just keep this to yourself at least until the kids are a little older and you'll have them on your own. Until then, you should be able to get away with hiding it. You were able to sneak around all that time at first with no problem."

"Alright, I've heard enough. This conversation no longer concerns me, so I'll be leaving."

"But you haven't even touched your food," Juliet said slightly.

"I lost my appetite; I'll find something later. I meant what I said, though, it's on you whether you'll be in your grandkids' life or not," I told her before getting up.

I walked over to the living room and put my coat on then grabbed my keys and purse. Chase was heavy on my heels trying to stop me, but there wasn't shit he could say to make me stay in his mother's house another minute. Juliet was lucky she was Chase's mother, or I'd have cursed her ball-headed, no-edge, Jenny off the block ass out. She's too damn old to be so god damn messy and in her grown son's business.

I opened the front door but before I could walk all the way out, Chase grabbed me by the arm gently and pulled me back in the house.

"Please, I need you to calm down before you leave. I don't want you driving home angry and wrap yourself around a pole. I'm sorry for my mother's behavior and I will talk to her. I promise the next time you see her she won't be like that."

"I don't need you to apologize for her, but you do need to talk to her because you know I don't tolerate disrespect. The next time I won't be so nice."

"Okay, don't stress about this. I promise I'll fix everything, and my mother will come around. Now drive safe and call me when you get home," Chase said. He pulled me into his arms and planted a kiss on my forehead.

"What the fuck is going on here?" a female voice screeched.

I turned around and was face to face with Diane. Me and Chase were so busy going back and forth that we never even noticed her walk in the house. This was just my luck. I should have followed my first mind and went home after my doctor's appointment instead of agreeing to this dumb ass dinner.

I looked up at Chase and his eyes were as big as saucers. He looked like a deer caught up in headlights. If I wasn't so pissed, I might actually have found humor in this shit. I had enough drama for one day though. I was hungry and my feet hurt, so I walked out the door and left Chase to deal with that shit.

CHAPTER ONE
DIANE

"What the fuck is going on?" I repeated again since Chase was standing there looking stupid. He looked like he was ready to run after McKenzie, but he was glued to his spot.

"What are you doing here?" Chase asked, looking at me then at his mother, as if that was more important than my question.

"I went to my doctor's appointment then checked on my aunt. Since I was out this way, I decided to come see your mom because I didn't want to be home alone."

"Did my mother know that you were coming?"

"No, I've never needed permission to come over before, so I didn't think I needed it now."

"You don't need permission, Diane. My house is always open to you no matter what," Juliet said solemnly.

I looked in her eyes and I could see guilt and sorrow in them. I couldn't tell if it was because she felt bad that I caught her lying ass son up or the fact that I caught McKenzie coming out of her house.

Chase ignored his mother's statement and pulled me out of his house. He held onto me until we made it to the side entrance, which was his front door. He took his keys out of his pocket and unlocked the door to his house and pulled me inside.

He walked to his bar and poured a shot of Hennessy then sat down on the couch.

"Why are you really here, Diane? You don't ever do pop ups over here without calling my mother first or without telling me."

I sighed then sat down on the couch next to Chase.

"Honestly, I came by because I wanted to see was you lying about going home to help your mom after your meeting. You didn't come home yesterday, and I just had a feeling like you were hiding something from me and from the looks of it, I was right. You're back fucking with McKenzie now? Is that why you've been acting strange lately? How long has she been back?" I asked question after question, trying to hold back my tears.

Chase ran his hand across his face as if he was struggling to decide on what he should say to me. It wasn't no point in him lying because McKenzie wasn't at his mother's house just for the hell of it. I walked in on the end of their conversation, and I could tell something had happened, but I wasn't sure what it was. I could tell from the softness in his voice and the way he kissed her on the forehead that he still had feelings for her. "It's not what you think, Diane. I don't—" Chase started, but I cut him off before he could come up with a lie.

"Don't sit here and lie to me, Chase. I saw McKenzie here after your ass lied about her moving to Miami."

"Shut the fuck up and listen. I'm not about to lie to you and I didn't lie about her going to Miami. She's been there for the past five months. She just came back out here last week."

"That still doesn't explain why she was with you. Is she back here for good? You didn't answer any of the questions I asked you."

"If you stop interrupting me, I can tell you."

"Fine, but please be honest with me. I can't take any more lies from you. I can handle whatever it is."

"Okay, so here's the thing. I'm not back fucking with McKenzie, but she's back here for good. The day I was shot, she came over here to talk to me. She told me that she's seven months pregnant with twins. I didn't come home and I've been acting strange because I didn't know the right way to tell you, especially since we lost our baby last month. McKenzie and I have no intentions of getting back together, but I do plan on being in my kids' life."

If felt like all the wind was knocked from my lungs as I listened to Chase talk. I said I could handle anything, but I was not expecting this shit. I would have rather he told me he was back sleeping with her. Here it was I lost two of our kids and he was having two more with another bitch. It was like he was replacing our kids.

"How the fuck could you let this happen, Chase? Not only were you cheating on me, but you weren't strapping up? Did you blow up with her when you found out she wasn't on birth control and got pregnant?" I yelled.

"I'm sorry, Diane, it wasn't like that. I'm not going to lie and say the condom broke or that she tricked me. We were having sex and she got pregnant. I didn't blow up on her or say anything because she's already seven months pregnant. I had already missed out on most of her pregnancy, and I didn't want to miss out on the rest."

I couldn't believe how Chase was just sitting here talking so openly and honest with me. I mean, damn, I asked for honesty, but I wasn't expecting these answers. There was no turning back now. I needed to know everything while I had the chance.

"Did you know all along? Is this why you didn't want our son? Is that why you weren't fazed by our son dying because you had new mutts on the way with that bitch to replace him?"

I regretted my words the moment they left my mouth. Chase's eyes turned dark, and I could tell he was about to get in my ass.

"Watch your fucking mouth. I get that you're upset, but don't you ever in your life allow some disrespectful shit like that to come out of your mouth while talking to me. If I ever hear you call my kids a mutt again, I'm going to hit you in your god damn mouth. Just because I didn't want you getting pregnant didn't mean I wouldn't love my child. I came back home and agreed to work on our relationship for the sake of the baby, so don't say I didn't give a fuck, and I just told your ass I didn't know about Kenzie's kids until a week ago!" Chase bellowed.

"I'm sorry, Chase, you're right. I shouldn't have said that. It's not the kids' fault who their mother is. So, what does this mean for us now? You're leaving me to be there for her and her kids?"

"No, I'm not leaving you for her, but I do think we should take a break. You're not going to trust me, and I can tell that you're hurt by her being pregnant. I can't keep hurting you like that. You deserve a lot better than the way I've been treating you. I'm not trying to argue with you every day about something I can't change."

My heart broke hearing Chase ask for another break from our relationship because of McKenzie. I hated that she was giving him something that I wasn't able to but at the same time, I loved Chase and I couldn't imagine my life without him, even if that meant accepting his kids.

"Please don't leave me, Chase, I can accept your kids. It's going to take time, but I promise I'll be there to help you with them, and we can continue to work on our relationship. If you say it's over with you and McKenzie, then I believe you," I cried.

Chase sighed then wiped the tears from my eyes.

"Stop crying, I'm not going anywhere. I can still sleep in the same house with you but in a separate bedroom. I'm not doing this to hurt you. I'm doing it to help you. You say you accept them, but I know it won't be easy for you. I'm giving you time to really think. Once they're here we can revisit this conversation to see if you still feel that way."

I hated that Chase would be sleeping in a separate bedroom, but I loved the fact that he'd at least be in the same house with me. That meant he wasn't completely giving up on us. I don't care what he says; I know that I'll be able to accept the babies. It's not like he started fucking with her again and got her pregnant. This was from when they were together back then, so to me it made a difference. I just hoped he wasn't lying about them not fucking around again. Or maybe that was the reason why he wanted to take a break, so he could have sex with her whenever he wanted without feeling guilty. At least then he wouldn't technically be cheating.

"Okay, what is she having?"

"A boy and a girl," he said with a slight smile. I could tell he was happy about it but was trying to hide his emotions to coddle my feelings.

"What was going on at your mother's house? Did she just find out about the pregnancy?"

"I'm not going to go into full details with you, but my mother found out the next day after I did. She knew McKenzie had a doctor's appointment today, so she invited her over for dinner and to discuss some things regarding the twins."

"Aww okay, so is McKenzie moving in here or something after she has the kids or are you helping her find a place? Does she plan on putting you on child support?"

"No, she has her own house already. I still haven't talked to her yet about how much money I'm going to give her a month. Right now, I'm playing everything by ear. I'm going to send her some money to start helping her get the kids' stuff and once I find out how much her bills are a month, I'll factor that into how much to give her."

"Okay, it sounds like you have it all figured out. Are you coming back to the house now with me?"

"Not yet, I need to go handle some things at one of my traps with my brother then I'll be home."

"Alright, I won't hold you up. I'm about to go home now. I'll see you when I get there," I said as I stood from the couch.

Chase walked me out to my car, then I drove home. I was lost in my thoughts the entire drive. I was wondering if Chase was really going to the trap or was he on his way to run up after McKenzie. I guess Chase was right about me not being able to trust him. I couldn't be mad if he was going to talk to McKenzie. She was pregnant by him after all, so that meant she was going to be in his life for the next eighteen years whether I liked it or not.

When I made it home, I parked in the garage then headed in the house. I made a salad then sat down at the table to eat. Chase's mother had cooked so I knew he had eaten already.

I loved Juliet, but I wondered if she knew everything her son was doing while smiling in my face acting like she didn't. Juliet had always been a mother figure to me but at the end of the day, she's Chase's actual mother and she'd always have his back. It had always been that way. Tino or Chase could do no wrong in her eyes, but I had a feeling that Juliet didn't care for McKenzie from the way she looked when I came over.

I finished eating, washed my dishes, then went upstairs. I took a long hot shower then climbed in my bed and turned on the TV. I silently cried as I clicked on the Netflix button. I scrolled through the shows and stopped on *13 Reasons Why*. I don't know why I picked this depressing shit, but I wasn't in a mood for comedy or drama. I was in a fucked-up mood and there was no going back from it.

I had no idea what I did to deserve a life like this. I gave my all to Chase and it's never enough. Maybe I need to do a makeover or lose weight. I mean, I'm pretty and I don't think I'm fat, but McKenzie was younger and beautiful as well with the perfect little frame. I don't understand how both of us could be his type, so it made me wonder which one of us really was. It seemed like he actually loved her and he's tolerating me.

I don't know how much longer I can keep up with this. I know family is everything to him. She's having his kids and there's nothing I can do about it. I can't compete with kids. I know agreeing to stay with Chase is like me welcoming a third person into our relationship.

Chase told me he doesn't plan on getting in a relationship with McKenzie again, but I know that doesn't mean he'll stop sleeping with her. As far as I know, he could be at her house right now in her bed while I'm sitting here depressed and crying my ass off.

I hate that I'm at home alone when Chase should be here consoling me and begging me to forgive him. His ass is the one that was in the wrong and he's making it seem like it's my fault. It's like he doesn't care about my feelings, and that's what pisses me off the most.

I was halfway through the episode when I heard the alarm go off. I jumped but relaxed once I heard it stop. I looked over at the clock and saw that it was nine. I smiled because Chase kept his word and actually came home.

A couple minutes later, I heard Chase coming up the stairs, so I laid down and played sleep. I didn't want him to think I was waiting up for him crying.

Chase staggered in the room and grabbed something from his drawer then went into the bathroom. He took a quick shower then came back into the room and sat on the edge of the bed.

"I'm so sorry, Diane, I know I fucked up. I don't know how to make this up to you, but I will one day. You don't deserve what I'm putting you through and I don't deserve a woman like you," he said before kissing me on the forehead then leaving the room.

Tears fell from my eyes after hearing Chase's words. In spite of everything Chase has done, I can't bring myself to hate him. I still love him more than anything. I was his first real girlfriend and his mother spoils him, so he's just misguided. I know eventually he'll grow up and do right by me because deep down, I believe he loves me just as much as I love him. He just doesn't know how to show it. If he didn't, he wouldn't still be taking care of me the way he does and he would have been left me.

CHAPTER TWO

BLAZE

I was sitting in the office of my warehouse smoking a blunt and signing paychecks for my workers. I had to pay my people that worked here at the warehouse and my employees at the studio. I have an office there but I'm mostly here all the time. I still needed to go over some paperwork for a possible club I'm looking to buy.

"Hey, we're going to the club tonight. Are you coming?" Josh asked as he sat down on the couch across from my desk.

"Nah, I got to go get my kids this weekend and I told Martez I'd help him finish McKenzie's kids' nursery before he goes home in a couple days."

"Well, aren't you nice. I still can't believe you be around that fine ass girl all the time and ain't tried to hit yet. Hell, I would have at least tried to get a taste or sample," Josh chuckled.

"It definitely takes some self-control on both of our ends, but that's my future wifey. I'm not rushing into anything with her, plus she's pregnant. We're going to do everything the right way," I replied seriously.

"That's what's up, but you know Kim and Tasia not going to make it easy for you."

"I'm not worried about them; they'll be cut off by then."

"Okay, if y'all need help with the room let me know."

"I'll keep that in mind, because I doubt we'll be done by the time Tez leaves."

"Alright, the guys on the dock are almost finished unloading the shipment."

"Cool, we don't have to unload it tonight though. We can do it Sunday morning when we come in since we need to count the money from the drops too."

"That's cool, don't forget your goddaughter's party is tomorrow."

"I didn't, I'll be there with the kids. If McKenzie's not tired, I'll bring her with me."

"Good, because Nita needs some female friends to hang out with so she doesn't always have to be up under my ass," Josh said, causing me to laugh.

Josh talked shit all the time about Nita always being up under him, but I know he loves that shit. She's the reason he's still living in Chicago. Josh is my right-hand man. I've known him since I was a kid. He was my brother's best friend and now he's mine. When he found out I was moving out here for college and expanding my family business, he moved out here with me from Cali.

Originally, Josh was supposed to be here for a year or so to help me, but he met Nita a few months before it was time for him to leave. He stayed to see where things would leave them. Now here it is five years later, they're married with two kids. I needed the help anyway, so it worked out for me. I became cool with guys since I been here but none that I could trust on the same level as Josh. With the help of him and Mason, I built a multi-million-dollar empire out here.

Business is only getting better ever since I started working with Martez. That was the best decision I could have ever made business wise and personally. If I never would have started working with Martez, I never would have gotten close to McKenzie. Then again, I still would have gotten close to her because I would have eventually met her through Lauren.

Josh stayed and helped me with some work so we both could get out of there. We were almost done when there was a knock on my door. I looked up and saw Kim standing in the doorway with a red mini dress on and a black pair of thigh-high boots. She walked slowly over to me and sat on the edge of my desk. She crossed her legs, and I got a full view of her pussy. The sight of it made my dick jump, but I wasn't fucking with Kim like that. She had been acting crazy lately, so her ass is on punishment.

"Kim, what are you doing here?"

"I wanted to come see you so we can spend some time together before I go out. I haven't seen you all week, haven't you punished me enough?" Kim pouted as she opened her legs then recrossed them.

"Uhm, that's my cue to go. I'll see you tomorrow, bro," Josh said as he got up from his seat and walked out of my office.

I put my ink pen down and sat back in my seat while looking up at Kim.

"I don't have time for that right now. I have to get ready and go get my kids."

"AKA, you going to fuck Tasia tonight," Kim stated sarcastically.

"If you stopped acting crazy you could join us one day. You know I'm not attracted to crazy. That shit doesn't make my dick hard."

"I know and I'm sorry, it's just when that random girl

answered your phone I was pissed because that meant you had blown me off for somebody else."

"She's not random, Kim, and it's not even like that between me and Kenzie. She's my friend and I'm just looking out for her, but I'm not going to lie and say I don't have feelings for her because I do. I just haven't acted on them yet."

Kim frowned at my words and rolled her eyes.

"Whatever, I'm not trying to hear that. When can I get some dick?" Kim asked, brushing off what I said.

"I'm busy for the next couple days. I got you though."

"Your loss, I need to go meet up with my girls. I'll call you later," Kim said.

Kim jumped off my desk and blew me a kiss before walking out of my office.

I shook my head and finished up the last of my work then left my office. I checked to make sure everyone was good then I headed to Tasia's house to get my daughter.

I knocked on the door and Tasia swung it open. I followed her into the house, and I couldn't keep my eyes off her fat ass. She had on a black, short, fitted dress that barely covered her ass.

"Where you about to go?" I asked as I closed the door.

"None of your business, you were supposed to be here an hour ago," she replied as she walked toward the back of her apartment to her bedroom.

"I told your ass I had business to handle, now answer my fucking question."

"I'm going to the club with my girls. You're keeping Kayla the full weekend, right?"

"Yeah, I'll bring her back Sunday morning. Where is she right now?"

"She's taking a nap, so that means you can give me some dick," Tasia said as she stood in front of her mirror applying a thick coat of makeup. I had nothing against females that wore makeup, but I hated when that shit was caked up. A bitch would hug you and her whole face print would be left on your shirt. Tasia was a decent looking female, so I didn't know why she was always on this ghetto shit.

Tasia is brown skinned, 5'6, 170 pounds with a flat stomach and big ass. She always has her hair in a different color weave or braids that damn near touched her ass. She was the true definition of a ghetto girl. She has a smart mouth and a fucked-up attitude. I met her a few years back on one of my blocks and we started fucking around. I would leave drugs at her house, and she'd go on runs with me until she got pregnant with our daughter. After that, I stopped getting her involved. I tried to move her up out of the hood and into a house, but she wasn't having it. The only thing she allowed me to do was move her into a bigger apartment.

"Come get it," I told her as I pulled down my jeans and boxers.

Tasia walked over to me and dropped down to her knees, placing my semi-erect dick in her mouth. I held the back of her head while she deep throated my dick. I felt like I was about to cum, so I stopped her and put a condom on. I turned her around and bent her over the edge of her bed.

I slammed my dick inside of Tasia and grabbed a handful of her hair as I delivered deep stokes.

"Awe shit, Blaze, damn, you're going to pull my hair out," Tasia cried.

I ignored her pleas and gripped her shit tighter. I gave her more than enough money, so she could afford a better weave.

"Shut the fuck up and cum on this dick," I demanded as I slapped her on the ass.

Tasia threw her ass back on my dick and I shook her ass cheeks, causing them to jiggle as my dick disappeared.

"I'm cummming," Tasia moaned as she came all over my dick.

I had a few more strokes in me, then I pulled out and took the condom off.

"Come suck me dry," I ordered.

Tasia dropped to her knees without hesitation and took my dick in her mouth. All it took was a minute before I was releasing my load down her throat. Once she was done, she opened her mouth to show me she swallowed every drop.

"Delicious," she said, licking her lips, causing my dick to jump. If I didn't need to go get my son, I would have bent her ass over and got ready for round two.

"Go put Kayla's stuff on while I go get cleaned up. I need to go get Marquis before Tameka goes to work."

I walked out of Tasia's room and into the bathroom. I grabbed a towel from under her sink and washed it with some soapy water. I'd take a shower later on at McKenzie's house once I finished helping Tez.

By the time I finished cleaning myself up Tasia was already standing by the door with our daughter and her bag. I looked at my daughter's head and I immediately got pissed off.

"Before you get mad, I combed her hair last night and she messed it up," Tasia told me as if she could read my mind.

"I don't give a fuck. She was here with you all day today and you knew she was coming with me. Just go get her hair stuff and I'll get somebody else to comb it since you can't do your job as a mother and make sure it's done."

"Who the fuck you about to have comb my daughter's hair? You better not be about to take her around no other bitch after you was just in here fucking me," she yelled.

"You better be lucky my daughter right there or I'd snatch your ass up for talking to me like that. You know by now that I don't take my kids around random people. Don't worry about who's going to comb her hair. She's not going with me tomorrow looking like that, so either go get the shit so she can get her hair combed or I'm leaving her here with you now and I'll get her in a few days."

Tasia rolled her eyes and stormed off without saying anything else because she knew I would leave Kayla for real, and that would mess up her plans to go hoe around with her friends this weekend.

Tasia came back in a couple minutes later with a popcorn can that I'm assuming had everything I needed for her hair. If it wasn't, I'm sure Kenzie would have whatever else I needed.

I picked my daughter up and left out of Tasia's house. I strapped her in her car seat then took the thirty-five-minute drive to Tamika's house. I called Giordano's and placed an order so it would be ready by the time I was done getting my son.

I pulled up to Tamika's house and parked in her driveway. I got my daughter out of the car then walked up to the door and rang the doorbell. I waited about a minute until the door was swung open.

"Hey, baby daddy," Tamika spoke.

"Hey, baby mama, is Marquis ready?"

"Yeah, come in, he's getting his bag."

"Where's your husband?" I asked as I walked in the house.

"He went to drop Adam off at his mother's house. We're driving out to Kentucky tonight since his cousin's wedding is tomorrow, but we'll be right back on Sunday."

"Okay, just a heads up, I'm not going home tonight. I'm staying at McKenzie's place just in case Marquis tells you he was at a girl's house." My son was one of those kids that you couldn't do anything around without him telling. He was always volunteering information just to have something to talk about.

"Alright, are you going to get her to comb Kayla's hair? If not, I can do it for you right quick."

This was one of the things I loved about Tamika. She was the total opposite of Tasia. She was unproblematic and a sweetheart. We got along better now as friends as opposed to being in a relationship together. Had I met her now rather than when I was eighteen, we probably would have had a better relationship since I don't travel as much anymore, and I have more help so that I don't have to stay outside all day and night. She was one of my best friends, kind of like McKenzie only I don't fantasize about how many ways I could make her cum without even penetrating her. We haven't had sex since our son was about three months old.

Don't get me wrong now, Tamika is a beautiful woman, I just wasn't attracted to her in that way anymore. She actually looked better than Tasia. She was prettier in the face, and she had a better shape. She was tall with a dark-brown complexion, brown eyes, a short pixie haircut, thick thighs, and a slim waist. Call it me being mature, but I respected her friendship and marriage, so all of us got along.

"Thank you, but I'm going to ask McKenzie to do it for me."

"Okay, tell her I said hi and make sure to send me the information for her baby shower."

"I will, and I'll have the invitation for you Sunday. Lauren and her friend Tori are sending them all out within the next couple of days."

Tamika knew about McKenzie from the beginning. She was my go-to for advice when I needed a female point of view. She was rooting for me to get with Kenzie. They talked on the phone a few times when I visited McKenzie in Miami and they ended up exchanging numbers.

Tamika said I had too much money not to have settled down by now, and I agreed with her. I was at the point in my life where I had everything I wanted except for a wife. I wanted more kids as well in the future. I'd give it a couple years and I'd be ready to move into a house that my kids and their future kids could be raised in.

I talked to Tamika for a couple more minutes, then I left with my kids and drove to get the food before going to McKenzie's house.

CHAPTER THREE
MCKENZIE

Tori and I were sitting on the couch playing catch up. I was letting her know about my day and what happened at Chase's house between the conversation with his mother and Diane showing up. Chase tried calling me, but I was in the shower and then right after that, Tori showed up, so I hadn't had a chance to talk to him yet about what happened. I didn't feel like talking to him about it tonight, so I'd talk to him tomorrow about it.

"Girl, now you got me rethinking sending her ass an invitation to the baby shower. She better act like she got some sense, because I'd hate to have to slap the shit out of her for playing with you," Tori said seriously.

Tori and I got along so well because our personalities were so much alike. We both looked like the quiet and innocent type but when rubbed the wrong way, we let it be known that we're not to be fucked with. It doesn't matter who it is, we don't back down.

"You don't have to worry about that. I told her about

herself, and Chase said he is going to talk to her. I plan on having a drama-free baby shower."

"You will if I can help you. We're going to celebrate your bundles of joy with style and grace." Tori smiled.

"I'm excited, I'm looking forward to what you and Lauren put together for me and I can't wait to see the nursery. Martez and Malakai won't allow me to see it until they're finished," I pouted.

Tori and I continued to talk until the sound of my doorbell went off. I was about to get up, but Tori stopped me.

"Don't get up, I'll answer it for you," Tori said as she got up from the couch.

Tori peeped through the window then opened the door. She stepped to the side and Malakai stepped in with his kids, bags, and pizza.

"Hey, McKenzie, this is Makayla and Marquis. Y'all, this is my friend I was telling you about," Malakai said as he walked over to the island and placed the food and drinks on the counter.

"Hey pretty girl, hey handsome," I spoke.

"Hey, you're pretty," Marquis said, causing me to laugh.

"Thank you, I see you get your charm from your father," I laughed.

"Yeah, you know I got to teach him young. Can you to do me a favor and comb Kayla's hair for me? Her mother gave me all the stuff that you need."

"Sure, but why didn't she do it? Didn't she know you were coming to get her?" I asked.

"I told her, but she felt like it was more important for her to get dressed and do her own hair for her to go out first."

"Okay, let me eat and then I'll do it for you."

"Thank you, is your brother upstairs?"

"Yes, he's up in the nursery doing something. I tried to peek in there, but he wouldn't let me."

"Alright, will they be good down here with y'all while I go upstairs and help him?"

"Yeah, we'll make sure they eat first then I'll put on cartoons while I comb her hair."

Tori walked over to the island and made plates for us and the kids. She helped them wash their hands then we all sat at the dining room together.

"Do you have a baby in your stomach?" Marquis asked me.

"Yes, I do, I have two babies in my stomach," I replied.

"My mommy had my brother Adam in her stomach, but not no more. He be at home crying a lot," Marquis said with a mouth full of pizza, causing Tori and I both to laugh.

"Can I drink?" Kayla asked, saying the first few words since she'd been here.

"Yes, make sure to eat your pizza too," I told her.

Once we finished our food, I sat and turned on *Mulan* while I started on Kayla's hair. Surprisingly, she sat still while I braided and put beads in her head.

"Everything is clean, is there anything else you need help with before I leave?" Tori inquired.

"No, but why don't you stay tonight? I don't know how long the guys will be and the kids will be going to bed soon. Plus, I don't like you driving to the city this late, which brings me to the other topic of discussion I have. I was wondering if you wanted to move in here with me temporarily. I know you were looking to get out of your parents' house, and I have more than enough space. I don't want to be here alone with only a couple months left in this pregnancy, and I know I'll need help with the kids once they get here. It's just an idea. I mean, I understand if you don't want to live with me," I rambled on.

"Relax, you're my best friend. Of course, I'd love to live here and help you with the kids. It'll give me a chance to save up money and get the hell from up under my parents. You can just tell me how much your bills are, and I'll help you monthly," Tori suggested.

"Yay, I'm so happy about this. It's just like we always wanted, even though kids weren't included in the equation."

"I know, but it'll be perfect because this house is huge. I'll talk to my parents tomorrow when I go home and start packing."

"Okay, you can have the guest bedroom up here down the hall. My father has the room on the first floor and my brother has the one in the basement. If someone else stays here, they can sleep on the couch in the basement, but I don't plan on having overnight guests like that."

An hour later, I was finished with Makayla's hair and putting a scarf on it. It was a little after ten, so Tori and I decided to bathe the kids and get them ready for bed since Malakai was spending the night here tonight. I didn't want to leave them in the guest bedroom downstairs alone, so I put them in my bed.

I stayed in the room with the kids until they fell asleep, then I got up and took a shower of my own. I stayed in for almost twenty minutes then moisturized my body and put on a pair of pajamas. I sat on my bed just as my phone went off. I looked at it and saw that it was Chase. I debated on whether to answer or not. There was no use in prolonging the conversation anymore.

"Hello," I answered.

"Hey, I was calling to see how you're doing. I'm sorry about what happened today."

"I'm okay, and it's fine. It was only a matter of time before you had to deal with it anyway. Diane showing up didn't affect me; that was all on you, buddy."

"You're right, but we're good. I sat down and told her everything. I didn't tell her about us sleeping together again, obviously, but I told her about the twins and that I plan on being in their life."

"Okay, and how does she feel about that?

"She claims that she'll accept them, and she wants us to stay together. I suggested we take a break so she can really think about what she's agreeing to. I'll still live in the house with her but in a different room."

"Why, so you can cheat in peace and if she asks, all you have to say is y'all not together anymore?" I asked.

"Why, are you volunteering for me to come share your bed with you?" Chase countered.

"Nope, that's why you don't have my address."

"That's okay, I'll have it soon. What you got going on tonight?"

"Nothing much, just chilling with Tori while my brother and friend work on the nursery."

"What else do you need for the nursery? I haven't bought anything for the kids yet."

"I'm not sure, they've been taking care of everything. You can just send me some money and after the baby shower I can buy whatever else is needed," I suggested.

"Nah, I'll transfer the money to your account tonight. I need you to calculate how much your bills are a month. I'll factor that in with how much money to give you every month to help you with the kids. I'd prefer for you to not work at least the first year of their birth and just focus on them and school."

"Alright, I'm fine with that. I'll send you the figures tomorrow."

"Okay, I'll talk to you later," Chase said before hanging up.

I put my phone away then walked down the hall to the guest bedroom. I peeked in and saw Tori in bed passed out already. I closed the door back then went back to my bedroom and turned the lights off. I was tired and I didn't want to wake the kids, so I didn't bother about turning the TV on. I closed my eyes and went to sleep instead.

At some point during the night, I felt the bed dip and I stirred awake.

"I'm sorry, I didn't mean to wake you," Malakai said.

"It's fine, what time is it?"

"Almost two, go back to sleep."

Malakai pulled me closer to him and rubbed my stomach until I fell back asleep.

The following morning, I stretched my arms and didn't feel anything. I opened my eyes and realized I was in bed alone. I looked over at the clock and saw it was almost noon. I stretched my arms then climbed out of bed and went to the bathroom. I released my bladder, brushed my teeth, and washed my face. I went downstairs and saw everyone sitting at the table eating.

I spoke to everyone then sat down with them. The table had pancakes, eggs, grits, sausage, and bacon laid out family style.

"Who got up and cooked breakfast?" I asked.

"Malakai was cooking when I woke up and I helped him toward the end," Tori said.

"Wow, y'all didn't have to do this," I replied as I made my plate.

"It's a thank you for yesterday. Are you coming with me and the kids to Joseline's birthday party still?"

"Yeah, what time is it at?"

"It's at three, so we need to leave here about two thirty."

"Okay, I'll be ready."

"While y'all are gone I'll be at my house talking to my parents and packing," Tori added.

"Tez, what are you going to do while everyone is gone?" I asked.

"I have some business to take care of today, so I'll be out most of the day, then after that I'll be back here finishing up the room since I'm leaving tomorrow night."

"Don't remind me, I'm going to miss you."

"I'll miss you too, but I'll be right back next month for the baby shower, and Pops, Lauren, and the rest of the family will be here as well."

We all continued to talk over breakfast then went our separate ways to start getting ready for the day. That was one of the perks of having so many bathrooms. Nobody had to wait around for someone to finish. My brother and father always knew that was something that irked my nerves, so they made it possible for me not to have that problem anymore. I felt like I could finally breathe in my house without any walls caving in.

I invited my mom, Tyrese, and Aniyah to come over tomorrow for dinner so they could see my house and we could try to clear the air some. My relationship with Tyrese hasn't been the same since the day I got into it with him for taking Chase's side, and I'm not sure what's going on with Aniyah. We talked off and on while I was in Miami, and I filled her in on some of the things that were going on with me, minus the pregnancy. I didn't want her having bedroom talk with Quan and telling him I was pregnant because there was no way he would have kept that to himself.

I tried explaining to her when I talked to her that was the reason I didn't tell her, but she was all in her feelings about the situation as if I was obligated to tell her everything. Hell, the father didn't know at the time, so it wasn't like I was broadcasting the shit. She made it seem like I was ruining my life by having these kids, as if she was the one I would call to watch them or needed to depend on her for support. She could barely watch herself from trying to keep up with Quan, so there was no way I would leave her with my kids anytime soon.

I loved my big sister, but I know first-hand how irresponsible she can be, and she has no room to judge me.

I snapped out of my thoughts and took a quick shower and got dressed in a black jumpsuit and a pair of black Uggs. Jumpsuits were the only thing comfortable to me. I hated maternity pants because the elastic left a mark on my stomach, and I wasn't wasting all that money on clothes that I'll never wear again anytime soon. I have no plans on having any more kids until my kids are at least three, and that's if I'm in a stable relationship at the time. I mean so stable that we're talking about walking down the aisle. I'm not trying to deal with two different baby fathers because I can already tell that Chase is going to be handful on his own, so the other baby father needs to be called husband. That's why I'm getting the IUD in my arm at my first appointment after the twins are born. You won't catch my ass slipping again, and I mean that.

CHAPTER FOUR

BLAZE

After I finished cleaning McKenzie's kitchen, I went upstairs to her bedroom and found her sitting on the bed with my kids fully dressed. I couldn't help but smile as I watched her sit and watch cartoons with the kids. I had the same warm feeling I had last night when I saw her with them. I was surprised to see her in bed with them sleep. I don't know why I expected to find them passed out on the couch or something.

McKenzie had actually bathed my kids and put them to sleep without me even having to ask her. I loved seeing her interacting with them. I can already tell that she's going to be an amazing mother. Marquis couldn't stop talking to me about her this morning while I was making breakfast.

Martez and I sat and talked yesterday while we were setting up the nursery. He wanted to know what was really going on between McKenzie and me. It was the same question my family and friends wanted to know as well. I tried to explain it to them, but it's kind of hard for me to explain the feeling I have to them when I'm around her. I guess in a way it's not their business and it's not meant for them to understand. None of them thought I could be serious about pursuing her because everyone knows I only date females the same age as me or older.

Tasia is a couple months older than me, Kim is two years older, and so is Tamika. Even the women that I've had sex with or just dated were never less than a year younger than me because I can't deal with immature women. I don't care how fine they are; if they're immature or don't know what they want to do with their life, I don't have time for it. I'm not into grooming women into being the way I want them to be. I need my woman to have a backbone and be my equal not my foot stool.

Don't get me wrong now, I know that McKenzie still has some growing up to do. I still can't explain what made me approach her because typically I would walk in the other direction if I saw women fighting. Her beauty caught my attention, though, and I couldn't resist. I had to know what the hell could have a woman that beautiful out in the mall fighting. I was hoping that she wasn't a ghetto girl because that wasn't my type at all. I dealt with enough ghetto shit when it came to Tasia.

I think what made me want McKenzie so much was the fact that she didn't sweat me. She had actually turned me down, and that was something I wasn't used to. I'm glad that I'm actually putting in effort and getting to know her. Even though she's five years younger than me, she's mature for her age and my kids like her already, so that's a win in my book. The same way she's willing to accept my kids, I'm willing to accept her. We have a ready-made family already.

The only thing left was for McKenzie to stop sleeping with her baby daddy. I can't push the issue on that right now, though, because it's not like I'm celibate. I know that I'll be able to trust Kenzie not to cheat on me when the time comes and vice versa. Right now, we're just getting all of the bullshit out of our system so that when we made it official, we could give each other our all.

"Are you going to just stand there like a creep looking at us or are you going to get ready so we can go?" McKenzie asked, breaking me away from my thoughts.

"Yeah, my bad, give me twenty minutes and I'll be ready."

I walked over to my dresser and grabbed some clothes then went inside of the bathroom to take a shower. I usually wouldn't get dressed in the bathroom, but my kids were out in McKenzie's room, so I didn't want them to see me naked.

I took a ten-minute shower, dried off, and got dressed in a pair of black Balmain jeans, a white long-sleeve shirt, and a pair of black and white high-top Giuseppe Zanotti sneakers. Once I was finished getting dressed, I walked out of the bathroom and dropped my dirty clothes in the laundry basket.

I put on my watch, diamond cross chain, and diamond earring in my ear then squirted on my Bond No. 9 cologne. I brushed my waves, and I was ready to go.

"Come on y'all, I'm ready to go now," I told them.

"Finally," Marquis said dramatically, like he had been waiting for me a long time.

"Boy, come on before I leave you here," I replied to him before picking up my daughter.

McKenzie climbed out of bed and grabbed her purse then waddled out behind us.

We walked down the stairs and put our coats on, then we were out the door.

I helped my kids into the back seat of my Range and helped McKenzie inside of the front seat before climbing in myself.

I allowed McKenzie to control the music like always as I

drove to Main Event. She was playing some type of Kidz Bop music that I never heard her play before.

"Why are you playing this?" I asked.

"Uhm, there's two kids in the back seat. I didn't know what kind of music y'all play around them. They're at the age where they both are sponges," she said as if the reason was obvious.

"You're right, ma, I need to pay more attention to that," I replied.

I know Tamika has it where our son doesn't listen to certain music because she nor her husband play it. Now Tasia, on the other hand, doesn't care. She has all types of shit going on at her house. That's why I be trying to get my daughter as much as I can.

I don't talk down to Tasia, though, because I know she loves our daughter and she's just raising her the only way that she knows how. She practically raised herself growing up because her mother was always in the streets chasing behind a man and her father would rather bathe in gin than make sure she was well taken care of.

When people found out Tasia was pregnant by me they all assumed she was trying to trap me, but that thought never even crossed my mind. Tasia was devastated when she found out she was pregnant with our daughter. She wanted a baby just about as much as someone wanted a root canal.

Tasia might be a hot girl, but she ain't out here fucking raw. We'd been having sex for years and I strapped up every time. That's something we both agreed on.

If I don't plan on being in a relationship with a person, I make sure to use protection. I'm not trying to have a bunch of baby mamas and mini me's running around here. I want one more child, but I want to share it with my wife. Two baby mamas are enough for a lifetime.

I pulled up to Main Event and we all got out of the car and

headed inside. I looked around until I found the section that Nita, Josh, and some kids were sitting in.

I walked over and introduced McKenzie to everyone, and Nita instantly embraced Kenzie and made her feel welcomed.

"I have game cards for everyone, and the food will be out in about forty-five minutes," Nita said.

"Okay, you can give McKenzie my game card and I'll use the kids' cards with them," I suggested.

"No need, Josh told me she was probably coming so I got her one just in case."

McKenzie and I took the game cards then found games for the kids to play. Marquis and Kayla wanted to get on a motorcycle ride, so I got on with Marquis and Kenzie got on with Kayla since she's smaller. I made sure to put her on so she wasn't on her stomach.

Josh sent a text letting me know the food was set up so once we got off the ride, we were headed that way when I heard somebody call my name.

I turned around and saw that it was Tasia and her hood rat friends. I could already tell she was about to cause a scene, and she knew I didn't play that shit.

"What the hell is this, Blaze? You out here playing family with this bitch and my child? You got a baby on the way and didn't tell me? Does she know we just fucked last night?"

I looked around and saw there were people looking at us, and McKenzie looked uncomfortable. I could tell she was debating on saying something and the last thing I wanted was her in here arguing while she was pregnant.

"Can you go take the kids to eat for me while I take care of this?" I asked McKenzie.

"Yeah," she answered reluctantly.

"Don't be sending my child with that bitch. I don't know her," Tasia snapped.

I had heard enough of Tasha's mouth. I grabbed her by the arm and pulled her until we made it outside.

"I don't know what the fuck your problem is, Tasia, but we don't do this shit. You know I don't involve people in my business. You've never gave a fuck about who I was with before so why you out here showing your ass now like you some scorned woman when we've never been in a relationship together?"

"Well usually you're not out parading my child around with the bitches like some big happy family. Why didn't you tell me you had a baby on the way?"

"If you see me out parading her around with my kids that means she's someone important, and that's not my baby. Even if it was, it's not your damn business. I don't say shit about who you fucking with, so stay the fuck out of my business. Don't you ever in your life pull some shit like this again. Out here showing your ass arguing with somebody that's pregnant. You're too old for this bullshit you're pulling."

"Just because you're with that young ass girl now, don't be throwing my age into this," Tasia snapped.

"Shut the fuck up, that's beyond the point. Get your friends and go back about your business. I'll be dropping Makayla off tomorrow," I said as I turned to walk away, but she grabbed me by my arm.

"You're not dropping her off tomorrow, I'm taking her with me now," Tasia yelled.

I snatched away from her and grabbed her by the arm.

"Stop playing with me, Tasia. This is my weekend with her and you're not cutting it short because you want to be petty. You know I don't play when it comes to my kids. I'm trying my best not to put my hands on your dumb ass. You know I will take you to court if you keep playing me."

"Okay, damn, I'm sorry for the way I reacted. I'm just not used to you having her around anybody except for Tamika."

"Well get used to it, because McKenzie is going to be in my life, and don't disrespect her again. Her name is McKenzie or Kenzie not bitch, so don't ever address her as that again," I told her before walking away.

I walked back inside and went back to the section where the group was. Everyone was sitting around eating. I made my plate then sat in the chair next to McKenzie. She was smiling and talking to Marquis and Nita. I couldn't tell if she was upset or not. I wasn't going to bring it up now with a group around us, but I'd discuss everything with her when we got back to her house.

Once all of us finished eating, the kids played a few more games and we picked out prizes. We sang happy birthday and ate cake, then we left. I knew a lot of walking around caused Kenzie feet to swell and I wanted her to feel comfortable.

We said our goodbyes and McKenzie exchanged numbers with Nita, then we were on our way.

The car ride home was quiet because the kids were knocked out and McKenzie was nodding off.

"Is it alright if we stay one more night? I'm trying to finish up this room with Tez and I don't want to drive the kids home late."

"Sure, I don't mind. I like having them around."

"Oh, just them?"

"You know I like having you around too."

I parked in McKenzie's driveway, and we went in the house. Since the kids were already sleep, we changed them into their pajamas then put them to bed.

"Come sit down for a minute so we can talk," I told McKenzie as I sat on her bed.

"We don't have anything to talk about. I'm not mad about what happened."

"You might not be mad, but I still want to apologize. I

checked her for that shit she pulled, and it won't happen again. I don't even know why she's acting like that."

"It's fine, I understand. We're good, I'm not holding what happened against you," she reassured me.

"Okay, I'm about to go help Tez."

"Alright, I'm about to shower and watch TV."

I left McKenzie's room and went to the nursery. It was coming along good. We painted the room in a nude color and all the furniture was white. We had put the cribs together already and set up the dressers. We still needed to do the changing tables and stock all the stuff Tez and her father bought. At the rate they were going, once the baby shower came McKenzie wasn't going to have anywhere to put the stuff.

"How was the party?" Tez asked.

"It was cool, the kids passed out and your sister about to be right behind them."

"Look, I was skeptical about this friendship or whatever you have going on with McKenzie at first, but I'm happy she met you. It makes me more comfortable while I'm in Miami to know she has you here to look after her."

"That's my lil' baby, I'll always do whatever is needed to look after her. Even when you go home, I'll still do drop-ins to make sure she's good and she ate."

"I'm glad to hear that and so is my father. We really didn't want her coming back out here after everything that happened, but we can't force her to do what we want. At the end of the day, it's her choice and we'll always respect it."

Martez and I continued to talk while we did the finishing touches on the room. About two hours later we were done, but neither of us was tired so we went down to the basement to have a couple drinks and play pool to kill time.

Martez got tired of getting his ass kicked so he called it a night. I wasn't about to play by myself, so I went back upstairs to McKenzie's room and took a shower then joined her and my kids in bed. I wrapped my arms around her and inhaled her hair before closing my eyes. I could definitely get used to going to sleep with her every night. We only had a few months left then my dream would finally come true.

CHAPTER FIVE

CHASE

I t'd been a month since everything went down at my mother's house. I barely talked to Kenzie on the phone. I only saw her once last week, and that was for her doctor's appointment. She met me at the clinic and then she went right back home. I asked her to come have lunch with me, but she denied it and refused to go back to my place with me. It's back to strictly talking about the kids and pregnancy only.

McKenzie text me to confirm the details for the baby shower for next week and I sent her ten thousand dollars to do whatever she wants with it right now, and I'm going to send her five thousand a month once the twins get here. I don't want her to have to stress or worry about money. I'm hoping with that amount of money it'll make her rethink having to rush and find a job, because I don't want my kids in daycare. Not at least until they can talk so they can tell us if something happened while they were away.

I picked my phone up from the nightstand and called McKenzie's phone for the fourth time today. She wasn't answering my calls and I'm not sure why.

"Why do you keep calling me, Chase?" McKenzie answered.

"Damn, that's how you answer the phone?"

"Yeah, when you keep blowing up my phone. What's so important that you have to keep calling and not send a text?"

"I was calling to check and see how you're doing."

"I'm good, I've been busy all day. You could have text and asked me that."

"Busy doing what?" I asked.

"Kenzie, come eat your food while I run you a bath," a male voice said in the background.

"Who the fuck is that at your house?" I yelled.

"I have to go, I'll text you later," she said before hanging up, completely ignoring my question.

I took my phone off my ear and looked at it. I couldn't believe she had just hung up on me, and who the fuck is this nigga I'm always hearing in her background? Her ass ain't slick at all. This why the hell she didn't want to give me her address because she doesn't want me seeing him with her.

I'm not about to sit here and go crazy trying to wonder what the hell is going on with her. If she wants to be sneaky and not tell me what's going on, I'll figure it out myself. I dialed Quan's phone and he answered it on the third ring.

"Yoooo," he answered.

"What's up, are you with Aniyah?"

"Yeah, what's going on?"

"Let me speak to her right quick," I said.

I heard shuffling in the background before Aniyah was on the phone.

"Hey Chase, what's up?" she asked.

"Hey, do you have McKenzie's address?"

"Yeah, why?"

"Can you give it to me?"

"Uhm, I don't know if I should. If she wanted you to have it, she would have given it to you."

I wasn't trying to hear that shit Aniyah was talking.

"Come on now, I be looking out for you and Quan when y'all be needing somewhere to lay up. Do me this solid and I'll give you $100."

"Okay, I'll text it to you but don't tell her I gave it to you."

"Okay, I won't, good looking out," I stated before hanging up the phone.

I looked at the time and saw it was already five. I didn't come home until almost four in the morning, so I spent most of the day sleeping and watching TV.

Since Diane and I are only supposed to be roommates, I try not to do things to confuse her into thinking I wanted more. I'm a man with needs and I'm not going to lie and pretend like I don't still love her or that I'm not attracted to her anymore. I push back temptation and don't touch or kiss her. We have simple conversation when we see each other, but that's not often.

Most nights I stay out until I know she's sleeping before going in the house. I'll stay in my room until it's time for her to leave out for work and I'd be right back out before it was time for her to get home.

Diane calls me throughout the day and sometimes I answer and sometimes I don't. She'd call and ask what I want for dinner, what time I was coming home, or what I was doing. Depending on my mood would determine what I actually told her. I didn't like being questioned because it was like being in a relationship still.

I wasn't out fucking around or running wild every night like she thinks. I've been focusing on work and getting prepared to be a father. I got head a couple times from one of my workers that I fuck with off and on, but that was about it. I haven't had actual sex with another female since the day I had sex with McKenzie. I've been tempted, but I just don't feel right having sex with other women while I'm having sex with McKenzie, even though it's been a month and she's made it clear that we will never be together again. It might sound crazy, but I'm still holding on to a little bit of hope that she'll change her mind. That's one of the main reasons why I suggested Diane and I just be roommates. If McKenzie decided to give me a second chance, I wanted to do it right this time. I would ask McKenzie about us again a couple months after the twins are born. If she still says she doesn't want to be with me, then I'll go back and work on things with Diane

I went in the bathroom and took a quick shower then got dressed in a pair of black jogging paints and a red long-sleeve shirt with a pair of red and black Air Max. I put on a couple squirts of my Armani cologne then put on my diamond chain with my earring and was ready to go.

I grabbed my car keys, wallet, and phone then left the house. I put McKenzie's address in my GPS and saw that it was twenty-five minutes away from me.

> *"Gotta come twenty if you hoppin' in the Benz*
> *Young turnt nigga from the D to the A*
> *I'm rockin' with the Lions*
> *Yeah, I'm rocking with the Braves*
> *Yeah, yeah, yeah, yeah, yeah, we paid*
> *Yeah, yeah, yeah, yeah, yeah, we paid"*

I rapped along to "We Paid" by 42 Dugg and Lil' Baby as I drove to McKenzie's house.

I pulled up to a nice ass townhouse with a Bentley truck in the driveway. I looked down at my phone to make sure Aniyah gave me the right address. I knew McKenzie's people had money but not enough to set her up in a house like this.

I got out of the car and rang the doorbell. A couple minutes went by before the door swung open.

"What are you doing here?" Tori asked.

"I'm looking for McKenzie. This is her house, right?"

"Yeah, but you weren't invited so you shouldn't be here," Tori replied.

"I'm not trying to hear that shit. Is she here or not?" I yelled.

"I don't know who the fuck—" Tori started but was cut off by McKenzie.

"It's fine, Tori, let him in," McKenzie called out.

I pushed past Tori and walked inside of McKenzie's house. Her shit was fully furnished with portraits and expensive looking furniture. I don't know what I expected to see when I went to her house, but it wasn't this, being that she just moved here about a month ago.

My brows furrowed and I saw red when I saw McKenzie sitting on the couch with some nigga sitting by her massaging her feet.

"What the fuck is this? This why you not taking none of my calls? You busy entertaining some other nigga," I shouted.

"Hold the fuck up, don't you dare come in my house talking crazy or questioning me. How do you even know where I live? I don't ask about what you got going on or dictate your pace, so don't you do it over here. We're not together anymore, so you don't have a say in what I do," McKenzie snapped.

"Fuck that, I'm not trying to hear that. You come back here and fuck me only to turn around and lie about you not fucking with nobody else. Maybe my OG was right. I might do need a DNA test for those kids. Ain't no telling what else your ass done lied about," I bellowed.

A look of hurt washed across McKenzie's face when those words left my mouth, and I knew I fucked up. I allowed my anger to get the best of me.

McKenzie got up from the couch, and the nigga got up with her.

"Your bitch ass doesn't get to call me a liar or a hoe. I was faithful to you the entire time we were together. I know how not to fuck around when I'm in a relationship, and I'm not a liar. I have no reason to lie to you or anybody else. You thought you was doing something by saying we fucked in front of him? That ain't shit he already doesn't know because I'm not with him. Don't call or text me until after my kids are born, then you and your bitch of a mother can get the DNA test y'all want so bad," she shouted.

"McKenzie, I'm sorry, I didn't mean that," I apologized.

"Come on, Kenzie, you don't have to deal with his shit," Tori told her.

"Did you tell him where I live at?" McKenzie asked her.

"Of course not, I would never do that. I don't even like the nigga." Tori shrugged, looking me in the eyes.

I couldn't help but chuckle at how bold that bitch was being. She's lucky I'm trying to change my ways, or I would have slapped the shit out of her when she first opened the front door talking crazy. I was about to say something else to McKenzie, but Tori pulled her arm gently and led her up the stairs, leaving me with Kenzie's company alone.

"Yo, it's time for you to go. Kenzie's pregnant with your kids and you're over here stressing her out, and that shit ain't cool."

"Nigga what? Who are you to tell me to get out of her house? Do you live here?" I asked.

"I'm Blaze, and I'm the nigga that's going to be playing stepdaddy to your shorties and piping your baby mama down." He smirked.

Before I knew it, I was running up on the nigga, but his ass was quick. He wasted no time punching me in the jaw. We were about the same height, but he was cockier. I wasn't worried about that, though, because I know how to hold my ground. I struck his ass back in his jaw, and we went blow for blow until Tori came running down the stairs.

"Would y'all nigga's chill, none of this is good for Kenzie. Whether y'all like it or not, both of you are a big part of her life. You're wrong, Chase, and you know it. McKenzie doesn't want you here so you should go. I'm sure once she calms down, she'll reach out to you. As for you, Blaze, McKenzie wants you to come here," Tori said.

There was a lot I had to say, but I had already put my foot in my mouth and made things worse, so I decided to leave. This wasn't the last of this though. Me and that nigga Blaze were going to definitely see each other again. I don't take his comment about playing stepdaddy to my kids and piping McKenzie down lightly.

I was pissed and needed a drink, so I drove to the city and stopped at the liquor store before going to the trap. I would've gone home, but I didn't want to take my anger out on Diane, and I didn't go to my other house because I wasn't in the mood to drink alone.

I parked in front of the trap then went inside. Some of my workers were bagging dope and weed, while the other ones were sitting around playing the game and serving crackheads through the side door. There were a few females sitting around drinking and smoking.

I walked back to my office and unlocked the door then sat on my couch. I had no intentions on doing any work tonight. I turned on the TV and kicked my feet up on the table before opening my bottle of Henny.

"Hey bro, I didn't know you was coming through tonight. I thought you would still be with Kenzie," Tino said.

"Yeah, I thought I would too. I went there and she was there with some nigga named Blaze and Tori. I was pissed and ended up telling her maybe Ma was right about me needing a DNA test. After that she went off on me and told me she doesn't want anything else to do with me until after the kids are born. Blaze felt some kind of way and said some shit to get under my skin. We ended up boxing it out before I left and came here."

"Man, you a dumb ass nigga, you know them kids are yours. Lil' sis wasn't even out in the streets like that. She was at work, home, or with you."

"I know, I was mad and regretted saying it as soon as the words came out of my mouth. I just hated how she was there with another man."

"The name Blaze sounds familiar. If it's the one I'm thinking of, he supplies half the south side with dope and runs a studio downtown that all of the celebrities use when they're in town and some more shit."

"It might be him; I know he got money because he had a Bentley truck sitting in her driveway, and we both know you got to have some kind of money to deal with her. Are you ready for your getaway?" I asked, changing the subject. I didn't want to talk about McKenzie and Blaze anymore.

"Yes sir, I dropped the kids off at Jennifer's mother's house already, so all that's left is for me to go pick her up then we'll be on our way to the airport. I have the ring and everything else will already be set up when we get there."

"That's what's up, bro. Sis deserves that ring you got for her."

"Yeah, I'm about to get out of here though. I'll text you when we land."

"Cool, can you tell Bri I said come here on your way out?" I asked.

Tino looked at me and shook his head before walking out of the room. I didn't care about him shaking his head. He could shake that motherfucker until it rolled off his neck.

I pulled my pants down and started jacking my dick as I waited for Bri.

"What's up, Bossman?" she asked when she walked in the room.

"This dick, now lock the door and come catch this nut," I told her.

Bri did as she was told then licked her lips before wrapping her wet mouth around my dick. I held the back of her head as she gave me some sloppy. She wasn't much in the face, but she was bomb on the head with a fat ass.

I felt like I was about to cum, but head wasn't enough. I needed to slide up inside of something, so I pushed her up and grabbed a rubber from my pocket and put it on. She wasted no time sitting on my dick and riding the shit out of it. It had been a while since I fucked Bri. Typically, she gave me head, but we barely fucked. She gripped my dick and touched her toes. I was on the verge of coming already.

I flipped Bri over and slammed into her from the back. I held onto her waist and covered her mouth as I beat her shit up. She was making too much noise and it was irritating me. Flashes of McKenzie fucking that nigga came to mind, causing me to fuck her even harder. I was taking all my anger out on her pussy until I was cumming.

"Fuck," I groaned as I pulled out of her. I grabbed a

hundred-dollar bill from my pocket and handed it to Bri. She pulled her pants back up and smiled at me before walking out of the room. There weren't any words needed because we both got what we wanted. I drunk a little more of my drink then stuck the rest in the bag and headed out so I could go home.

CHAPTER SIX

MCKENZIE

A week had passed since I had to kick Chase out of my house. He called and text me every day trying to apologize, but I wasn't trying to hear that shit. He and his mother could talk about me all they wanted, but what they won't do is pull my kids into it. Today is the day of my baby shower and I have no idea how it's going to go because Malakai will be there. I have a feeling it's going to be some bullshit since he and Chase already fought. The good thing is my father and brother will be there, so they're not going to let anybody ruin my day.

"Okay, I'm finished, do you need help getting dressed?" Charmaine asked as she ran her fingers through my curls.

"No, I should be good, but I'm going to need help putting my shoes on. I can't even see my damn feet."

"Alright, I'm about to go make sure your niece is dressed because Lauren will have a fit if we get there late," Charmaine said before leaving out of my room.

Charmaine spent the night with me last night so she could

help me with my hair and makeup because I was too lazy to do it myself or go somewhere to get it done. Aniyah was supposed to come over last night to help Lauren and Tori finish the last of the stuff for the baby shower, but she flaked out on them, leaving Martez and Malakai to help instead. I didn't care if she came or not, though, because I was still pissed that she gave Chase my address. It made me feel like I can't trust her and that she'd do anything for money. I wasn't allowed to help or see anything, so I was locked away in my room with my father and niece. It felt good having all of us under the same roof again. They're all staying here until the twins are born.

I've already been having Braxton-Hicks contractions and I'm dilated two centimeters. My doctor is estimating that I'll go into labor within the next couple weeks, so my father would rather be safe than sorry. There was no point flying all the way back to Miami then back out here two weeks later. All of his work could be done via the computer and so could Lauren's and Martez's. As far as the illegal business goes, that's what their right-hand men and other workers are for. They'll still have meetings with them, but it'll be via the computer.

I grabbed my beige strapless jumpsuit and put it on with the long-sleeve long jacket to match. I put my diamond heart chain with the earrings and bracelet. The color scheme for the baby shower was neutral, so everyone was supposed to wear brown, beige, or cream. I was tired just from getting dressed, so I sat down on the edge of the bed. Being pregnant was tiresome as hell. I was not doing this shit again unless I'm getting married and my husband wanted a child. I commend anybody that had two-plus pregnancies. My feet ache even without me walking, and I'm not going to even talk about my damn back. Then I can't sleep comfortably because all I can do is sleep on one side all night. When I switch sides to where the twins are, it feels like they have a soccer game going on inside of me.

"TT, you look pretty, do I look pretty?" McKenna asked.

"Of course, you look pretty, you look just like me, duh," I said, causing her to laugh.

"Why don't you have your shoes on?"

"I can't bend over to do it."

"I can help you," she said eagerly.

Kenna grabbed my beige wedges and did her best to slide them on my slightly swollen feet.

"TT, your feet too big. Do you have more shoes?" she asked, giving up.

"Charmaine will be in here in a minute and she can help you."

We waited a couple minutes then Charmaine came in the room dressed in a cream fitted pants suit with a pair of four-inch heels. Oh, how I miss being able to wear pumps. Even if my feet could fit in them right, my brother or Malakai wouldn't let me wear them anyway. I put some on a couple months ago and they made me change before I could get out of the house. Talking about I might trip and fall over my feet.

"Char Char, my TT feet too big for her shoes. She needs some new ones," McKenna told her. Leave it to my niece to say the first thing that came to mind. I'm glad I wasn't self-conscious about the situation, because this child could definitely humble you.

"Alright, Ken Ken, let me see if I can help her." Charmaine smiled.

Charmaine squatted on the floor and carefully slid the shoes on my feet. I was going to pack my slides, but I wanted to at least take pictures in my pretty shoes first.

"Thank you, Charmaine," I said as I stood to my feet.

"You're welcome, mamas, now come on, because your dad and brother are downstairs waiting on you. I'll grab your bag and phone for you."

I looked at myself in the mirror and smiled at the fact that I didn't look how I felt. I was at the point in my pregnancy where I didn't like putting on clothes. My wardrobe for the last couple of weeks has been tank tops, sports bras, and leggings or biker shorts. If I didn't have people in my house all the time, I'd walk around in my birthday suit. That's definitely how I sleep unless Malakai comes over and ends up falling asleep.

I walked down the stairs where my father and brother were sitting on the couch talking. They stopped once they saw us enter the room, which meant they were probably discussing business.

"Te ves hermosa mi hija," my father complimented me.

"Gracias, Papa," I replied.

"You do look beautiful, but I think you need to change those shoes," Martez added.

"Thank you, and my shoes are fine, Tez. I'm not going to keep them on all day. I just want to make an entrance in them and take a few pictures. Charmaine has my flats in my bag," I told him.

He looked like he didn't like my answer, so I pouted a little and he left the subject alone. I smiled inwardly because it worked every time.

We all walked outside and climbed in Malakai's Escalade. He was letting my brother keep it while he's in town so they didn't waste money on a rental. He and my father would be alternating between Malakai's truck and my Lexus.

Martez drove for ten minutes until we pulled up to a banquet hall. I had no idea where the shower was going to be held at, but I was grateful that it was close to home. I just hoped I could get through the entire event without needing to go home and get in bed. My family put a lot of time, effort, and money into the event, so I wanted to show them I appreciated it.

Martez helped me out of the truck, and we all walked inside. The hall was beautifully decorated and full of people already. There was a DJ and a bar with a couple of tables full of dessert and food. The decorations were amazing as well. I wasn't sure who they hired to decorate. There was even a floor wrap with my maternity pictures in the center of the dance floor. Up front were two chairs fit for a king and queen. The thing was, I wasn't even sure if Chase's dumb ass was going to show up let alone sit up front with me.

I walked around and greeted my guests, then a huge smile plastered on my face when I made it to the table where my family from my father's side was sitting. Lauren lied to me and told me they weren't going to make it, so I was a little disappointed about that because it meant I wouldn't be able to see them until the twins were at least three-six months, when it was safe to travel with them.

"Abuela, lo lograste." I smiled. (Grandma, you made it.)

"Por supuesto, mi querida nieta," she replied. (Of course, my dear granddaughter.)

My grandmother understood English, but she preferred all of her family to speak Spanish when talking to her and my father did the same sometimes, so I became fluent in Spanish. I know how to read it, write it, and speak it, making it my second language.

I hugged my aunts, uncle, and cousins as well before walking over to where my mother, my siblings, and my aunt Cathy were seated. I had no idea why Tori invited this nosey ass lady to my baby shower. I had nothing against her, but she gossiped too much for my soul.

"Hey baby, where is Chase?" my mother asked.

"I'm not sure, he should be on his way," I replied.

"You did invite your baby daddy, right? You're not going to be sitting in the front by yourself, are you?" Cathy asked.

"Yes, I invited him and even if he didn't show up, I wouldn't be sitting in the front on my own," I pointed out before walking away. She was already getting on my nerves.

I walked over to the final table in the front where Malakai, Nita, Tamika, and Josh were seated. I had no idea who they invited from Chase's family because it was only my friends and family here, and I was fine with that.

"Hey, thank you all for coming," I said to everyone at the table.

Everyone spoke back to me, and Tamika kept looking at me and smiling.

"It's so good to meet you in person. I can see why Blaze likes you so much," Tamika said.

"It's good to meet you as well."

"You're welcome, I told you I was going to be here and I'm a woman of my word."

"You look beautiful, but I'm going to need you to change your shoes," Malakai stated, just as I expected.

"I already had this conversation with Martez before I left the house. I want to take pictures first in the shoes then I'll switch over to my slides."

"Okay, well sit down while I go find the photographer for you," Malakai suggested.

"Yes, daddy," I mumbled as he walked away.

"Damn girl, you got my boy whipped and y'all not even together yet. I better enjoy hanging with him while I can, because once y'all together that nigga not going to want to leave the house," Josh half joked.

"Leave my brother alone, you're the same way right now and we've been together for five years," Nita said, putting her husband on blast.

I sat around and talked with the group until the door

swung open. I looked up and saw Chase, Tino, Jennifer, Quan, Tyrese, Aniyah, and Juliet. All I could do was shake my head. My own sister and brother couldn't be on time because they chose to come when Chase decided to make an appearance. I turned my attention back to the group I was talking to at the table. They couldn't bother about being on time, so I wasn't about to go out of my way to go speak to them.

A couple minutes later, Malakai came back and sat down next to me.

"Are you good? Do you need anything?"

"No, I'm fine, did you find the photographer?"

"Yeah, she's changing something on the camera. Do you want to take pictures at the backdrop or in your chair?"

"Can I take pictures in my chair at the backdrop?"

"Yeah, I'll move the chair for you. Come on so you can get this over with and change your shoes. They don't look like they're comfortable at all."

I sighed as I got up from my seat and walked over to where the photographer was. My feet weren't even bothering me, but I knew Malakai wasn't going to leave the shit alone and Martez would be breathing down my neck soon.

I sat down in the chair and the photographer took pictures of me by myself then some with Malakai as well. Lauren announced for the family of the mom-to-be to come take pictures. We took a big family photo then I took some with my abuela, dad, mom, and siblings alone.

Tyrese and Aniyah smelled straight up like weed, so I needed them to hurry up and get away from me because it was embarrassing and making me nauseous. I could only imagine how those pictures were going to turn out. Once I finished with them, Tino came over with Jennifer and he introduced us before I took a couple pictures with them. Chase or his mother didn't bother coming over to take pictures, and I didn't care. I know he's probably in his feelings because he saw Malakai here, but I didn't give a fuck. I wasn't about to turn my back on a friend that's been here for me because he's in his feelings.

Food and drinks were served then games were played. Everyone seemed to be having a good time laughing and dancing to the music that was playing. I was getting tired, so Lauren announced that it was time for me to open the gifts. I guess that's when Juliet's liquor kicked in, because she strolled over to the table where I was sitting with some of my family and Malakai.

"How the hell you invite my son here, but you got two other men here with you as well? I guess you really don't know who your baby pappy is," Juliet slurred.

I held my head down from secondhand embarrassment. If Chase knew what was good for his mother, he would come get her away from me. I respected her because she was Chase's mother, but that didn't mean shit to my family.

"Hija, quien es esta loca?" my father asked angrily. (Daughter, who is this crazy lady?)

"Chase's mother," I mumbled.

Martez jumped up from his seat and walked over to Chase and said something before Chase and Tino came rushing over to where we were.

"Come on, Ma, you've had too much to drink. Let me take you home," Tino offered.

"I'm not ready to go yet. I'm not finished talking to this lil' bitch right here," she said, dragging her words.

Before I could respond, my aunt Victoria jumped up from her seat and slapped the shit out of Juliet.

"You listen to me, and you listen good. I don't care who you are or how you feel, you will not disrespect my niece. If you don't know what's going on, you need to mind your own damn business. Your son is a grown ass man that can speak for himself. You're acting like you was in the bedroom with them when those kids were made," Aunt Victoria snapped as she pointed her finger at Juliet.

Juliet was still standing there stunned by the fact that my aunt smacked her and called her out on her bullshit.

"Yo, Chase, take your mother home and we'll forget this happened," Martez spoke in a no-nonsense tone.

"I apologize on my mother's behalf, McKenzie. I'll take her home. Let Chase stay here so he can see you open the gifts and cut the cake," Tino countered.

"I don't care who takes her home, but she needs to get out of here," my father added.

Tino grabbed his mother by the arm gently and led her to the table to get her coat, then they headed out the door.

"Okay, there's nothing to see, it's time to open up presents," Lauren called out over the mic.

"Can I sit up there with you, or do you plan on your lil' boyfriend sitting up there with you?" Chase asked sarcastically.

I whipped my head in his direction so fast I almost caught whiplash.

"You haven't said one word to me since you been here and then your mother shows her ass, and you have the audacity to want to be sarcastic with me. You're lucky I even let y'all up in here. I'm not in the mood, so don't play with me, Chase. You can sit up front with me if you want to, if not, I really don't care," I whisper yelled so only he could hear.

Chase sighed then followed me over to the stage. We opened presents and took pictures like we were a happy couple. I had so much shit that my kids were going to need another closet. Once we were done, I cut the cake and I was out the door with Charmaine. She was going to drop me off at home then come back and help get all my gifts and clean up. My feet, back, and head were killing me. All I wanted to do was take a long bubble bath then go to sleep.

CHAPTER SEVEN
ANIYAH

McKenzie's baby shower was three days ago, and I knew she was still upset with me for giving Chase her address as well as flaking out on Lori and Lauren when it came to helping with the shower. To be honest, I didn't have an excuse as to why I didn't go help them. I was busy running the streets with Quan. I guess I felt some type of way about Lauren and Tori throwing the shower for her when she's my sister.

McKenzie didn't think to call and tell me about her baby, yet Lauren and Tori knew from the beginning. I didn't find out until she came back to Chicago when she was already seven months pregnant. Yet again, she made a huge decision about her life and left me out. Granted, I didn't have a good job to pay for the kind of stuff they did, but I could've got it from Quan and at least had some input.

I was still in my feelings about McKenzie up and leaving for Memphis without telling me. I didn't know she was gone until I got home and my brother and mother told me what happened. I tried to call her but she was in the air. She called me back once she was already at her father's house. I tried to talk her into coming back but she wasn't having it. It was like I had lost my best friend that day.

I always thought I'd be the one to move out first since I was the older one. Quan was still dragging his feet with find us a place while McKenzie was living in that nice ass townhouse funded by her brother and baby father. Then, to make matters worse, she moved Tori in with her without even asking if I wanted to live there. It was like she forgot which one of us was her sister.

I love my sister, but sometimes I can't help but have a tinge of jealousy when I know I shouldn't because if I needed it, she would be willing to give me whatever I want. The thing is, I hate that there might come a time where I will actually have to put my hand out and ask for something from my sister. She had it made, and there wasn't anything I could do about it.

When I found out she was pregnant, I was like little miss perfect finally messed up, only for my mother to be happy she was finally getting grandkids. Honestly, I think my mother took it so well because she was just happy McKenzie was back in the same town and she didn't need her help to take care of her kids.

Only McKenzie could leave town heartbroken and pregnant then come back with a smile on her face and a man trailing behind her. When I saw Blaze, I was like god damn, Quan who? Only to find out he was next in line to be with McKenzie. The nigga didn't care about her being pregnant or anything. She had to have the best luck in the world because the only thing that happened to her was a nigga cheating on her and even still, that nigga was willing to leave his woman to be with her. She had two men with money fighting to be here with her while I'm stuck with Quan.

Don't get me wrong now, I love my man and his dirty drawers. I just wish he had more money in his pockets and was better in bed. He wasn't broke but he wasn't as well off as Chase or Blaze. If he was, we would have found a house a long time ago and it wouldn't be taking two years to save. He did give me money sometimes but it wasn't much. It was enough for me to buy some sneakers at Footlocker and a fit from Rainbow. If it was a good day I could probably throw in a full set as well.

I just don't get it. I'm a good girl with my head on my shoulders. I go to school and work. I listen to my parents and I don't run the streets. I've been with same guy forever and I know I got some good pussy, but it feels like I have to settle while McKenzie is the total opposite of me and she has the world handed to her on a silver platter.

McKenzie listens to her father but she's always been disobedient to our mother and talks back. She likes to go outside and run the streets. She done slept with like three or four niggas already and no one cares. It's amazing how one night could change a person's life.

Had my mother never been hot in the ass and got pregnant by a rich man, McKenzie wouldn't be living the life she's living right now. Hell, she might not even be here. Wait, I don't mean it like that. I'm just ranting because I'm in my feelings, and I feel like Quan is hiding something from me. I really do love my baby sister and I'd do anything for her.

I'd do anything to the point where I'm going to plaster a smile on my face and spend the day with McKenzie, Tori, Lauren, and Charmaine. God knows I can't stand Lauren, but I'm willing to bite my tongue to make things right with McKenzie. Lauren has never done anything to me personally. She just rubs me the wrong way. She's stuck up and has the tendency to look her nose down on people. McKenzie says I'm just tripping and that's how people are in Miami. I guess McKenzie doesn't pay attention to it because they're so much alike. Then Lauren thinks just because she's engaged to Martez that she's her sister. Always calling her sis and shit irritates my soul. McKenzie has one sister and that's me.

McKenzie had a few more things she wanted to get for the babies. Why, I have no idea, because she had got more than enough at the shower. People bought her expensive car seats, strollers, high chairs, and clothes. Whatever they didn't buy, Martez and her father had already bought for the nursery. She didn't have to spend a dime of her own money for anything.

McKenzie insisted on going, so I volunteered that we all get together when everyone is free. We're going to go to Rosemont Mall then out to dinner. It'll be our last outing until McKenzie has the twins. Once they're born, it's no telling when we all will be able to go out again.

"What is taking them so long?" I complained.

"Chill, your sister is pregnant so it takes longer to get ready. Tori said they were on the way out now," Charmaine replied.

I sighed because I had already been outside waiting for them for ten minutes. McKenzie chose the time and had the nerve not to be ready in time. I was ready to go and get this day over with. It was bad enough I had to drive forty-five minutes to come here to get them.

After waiting a couple more minutes, the girls came walking out.

"Hey y'all, sorry we're late, they were helping me get ready. I couldn't put my socks and shoes on by myself. Luckily Lauren threw these braids in my hair last night or it would've taken even longer," McKenzie apologized as she slid in the backseat with Tori and Lauren following her. They spoke as well then started playing in their phones.

"It's fine," I replied as I pulled off.

After driving for twenty-five minutes, we pulled up to North Riverside Mall.

"Girl, why are we here?" McKenzie inquired.

"You said you needed to shop for the twins. There's a Children Place, American Kids, and Foot Locker," I pointed out.

"Uhm, I'm not allowed in here after the fight I had. Plus, I need to go to a Target or an actual baby store. Let's just go eat at Chili's and I'll do a store pickup for the kids' stuff later," McKenzie said.

Honestly, I had completely forgot about them banning her from the mall.

I drove back out of the mall lot and drove up the block and parked at Chili's. It was only three so they weren't crowded at all.

We were seated as soon as we made it in the restaurant. The waiter took our drink orders and we all knew what we wanted so we ordered our food as well.

"So, are you ready to be a mama, Kenz?" Charmaine asked.

McKenzie's face lit up as she answered her.

"Yes, I am. I'm not going to lie and say I'm not nervous, but I can't wait to meet my little ones."

The five of us continued to talk over our food. Once the bill came I looked at it and was ready to pay for my portion. My food was only $13, Charmaine had a steak, McKenzie ordered two meals, Lauren had a meal plus an appetizer and so did Tori.

"Don't worry about it, it's my treat," little miss perfect Lauren stated as she pulled out her debit card.

I rolled my eyes before putting on a fake smile and thanking her. I wasn't too proud to accept a free meal. After Lauren paid the bill, we climbed in the car. It was still early so I offered to take McKenzie to Target to get what she needed.

During the drive my phone started ringing. I looked down at it and saw that it was Quan finally calling me back.

"Hello," I answered.

There was silence in the background, then I could hear moaning. I just knew I was tripping, so I turned up the volume on my phone and heard Quan talking. This nigga really had me fucked up. Instead of going to Target, I made a detour to the trap because that's where Quan is supposed to be.

"This isn't the way to Target or the house," Tori said after realizing the direction we were going.

"I know, I just need to grab something from Quan right quick," I lied.

I guess they believed me because no one said anything else.

I pulled up to the trap and saw Quan's car parked right out front. I climbed out of the car and walked up the stairs then knocked on the door. One of the guys opened the door without saying who is it.

"Hey, Aniyah, what you doing here?" he asked. That was strike one. They never questioned why I came here, but I played along.

"I'm here to see Quan," I replied.

"He's in a meeting right now," the worker stuttered. That was strike two.

I didn't have time to play with him, so I pushed past him and made my way toward the back of the house where the bedrooms were. I continued to walk until I heard moaning coming from a room, and that was strike three.

I twisted the knob and it wasn't locked, so I pushed the door open. Tears instantly filled my eyes when I saw a bitch on top of Quan riding his dick.

"What the fuck is this?" I yelled as I yanked her off of him. Quan looked like he wanted to crawl in a hole while the bitch he was fucking had a smirk on her face.

"Baby, I can explain," Quan said, jumping up and putting on his clothes.

"How could you do this to me?" I cried.

"Let your hoe ass sister know what it feels like to find out your man is fucking another bitch. Not only did she fuck my cousin's man, but she got pregnant by him. That was an all-time low, even for her," Shavon spat.

"Why would you do this, Shavon? I don't have any beef with you. Whatever happened between you and Kenzie had nothing to do with me," I pointed out to her.

"I'm sorry, but it is what it is. Your sister needed to be taught a lesson, and it wasn't like she had a nigga I could fuck for revenge." Shavon shrugged before putting on her clothes and walking out of the room.

I was too stunned to even chase after her. Out of all the bitches Quan could cheat on me with, he chose my stepsister.

"I hate you, Quan. I hope your dirty dick falls off for this shit. That's my fucking stepsister and you chose to sleep with her."

"I fucked up, baby, but I swear it wasn't planned. I came here to do some work and she was in the bed naked already. I told her to get dressed, but she wouldn't listen. She crawled between my legs and started massaging my dick, and I gave in," he explained.

"Fuck you and that bitch," I yelled before walking out of the room. I walked through the house and everyone was looking at me, but I ignored them. This shit was embarrassing as hell.

I walked outside and got in the car then pulled off.

"Is everything alright?" Charmaine asked.

"No, it's not. I just walked in on Shavon and Quan fucking."

"Damn, did you beat they ass?" Tori asked.

"No, I just listened to their explanation and walked out," I admitted.

"Are you serious? You actually saw them fucking and you ain't do nothing?" McKenzie inquired as if it was the craziest thing she'd ever heard.

"I didn't do shit because all of this your fault. She wouldn't have tried to fuck him had you not been fucking with Chase. I told your ass to leave that nigga alone, then you go and get pregnant by him," I yelled.

"Your ass must've inhaled some of that crack in that trap if you can sit here with a straight face and blame me for your nigga putting his dick where it don't belong. Even if she did come onto him because of me, his ass could've said no," McKenzie snapped.

"Fuck that, you're always doing shit that hurts other people and you never have to deal with the consequences. We always have to be the one to clean up your messes while you skip town when shit gets hard because you're nothing but a spoiled bitch," I shouted.

"Bitch, you got me fucked all the way up. You already know I don't even do this back and forth shit. The only reason I ain't swung on your ass yet is because you're driving and I'm pregnant. Don't play with me, Aniyah, because you've never had to clean up shit for me. I don't leave town because I'm weak or scared. I leave town because if I stay here, shit will get hella worse, and you know this. I'm going to let you slide, though, because you're my sister and you're in your feelings, but let that be the last time you call me a bitch or I won't be so forgiving," she threatened.

I was about to respond, but Charmaine cut me off.

"Aye, chill with that shit, y'all are sisters. McKenzie is right, though, Aniyah. Your anger is misplaced, baby girl. You should've picked up something and beat both of their asses," Charmaine said.

It was just like Charmaine to be the mediator and take McKenzie's side. I guess she forgot that I'm the one that's her real cousin and I was the one here for her when McKenzie skipped town.

I ignored everyone as I continued to drive. I didn't feel like going back and forth with them anymore.

I drove toward the e-way when my phone started to ring. I looked down at it and saw it was Quan. I hit ignore but he kept calling, so I finally answered.

"What the fuck do you want?"

"We need to talk? Are you on your way home?"

"None of your damn business. Go ask Shavon where she's on her way too," I said before hanging up the phone.

As soon as I hung up, he called right back and when I didn't answer, he sent a text.

"You have a lot going on right now. Maybe you should let me drive," Charmaine suggested.

"I'm good, it ain't nothing I can't handle," I assured her.

When I made it to a red light, I looked down at my phone and read his text.

Hubby: Please forgive me, I have a surprise for you.

I was in the process of texting him back with the light changed. I didn't realize it and cars started blowing their horns at me. I needed to be in the turning lane, so I jumped over.

"Nah, for real, you're about to cause an accident. Let me out this car and I'll Uber home," McKenzie said dramatically.

"Let me put my seat belt on," Tori mumbled.

All of them in the backseat did the same thing trying to be funny, but I wasn't in the mood so I ignored them and finished my text. I didn't realize the light had turned red when I hurriedly turned, and before I could complete the turn, a truck came flying toward us. I pressed on the brake, but I wasn't fast enough. The car hit the passenger side of my car, causing me to lose control and spin out, running into a parked car. My head hit the steering wheel and after that, everything went blank.

CHAPTER EIGHT

BLAZE

"That was a foul, it's my ball," Josh yelled.

"Man, that wasn't no damn foul. We ain't been calling fouls none this game and now you want to call one since y'all ass losing," Martez yelled back.

"Martez is right, shut the hell up and take this ass whooping," I chuckled before shooting the ball in the hoop.

Martez, Josh, and I took care of business earlier here at the warehouse. Since we haven't heard from the girls, we decided to play basketball in the gym here with some of the guys. We've been playing for almost an hour and I'm ready to quit, but these niggas keep talking about just one more game.

"Yoooo, Martez, somebody blowing your phone up," Nick called out.

"That's probably Lauren trying to see where your ass at. We been here long enough," I said.

Martez walked away to take the call. Two minutes later, he was rushing to put his shirt and coat on.

"Aye, we got to go. That was my pops, the girls were in a car accident," he said hurriedly.

I ran across the court and put my shirt and coat on as well. I grabbed my cell phone and put it in my pocket, then we were out the door.

"Let me drive y'all to the hospital. Neither one of y'all are in the right state of mind," Josh offered.

"Thanks man, you can keep my car and I'll get a ride to it once we figure out what's going on."

"Don't worry about that. I'm going to call Nita and she'll meet us up there."

The remainder of the car ride was quiet after that. I was lost in my thoughts during the deration of the drive. I could tell Tez was spaced out, and I couldn't blame him. His girl and his sister were in an accident together and we had no idea how they were doing.

Josh found a park and we all got out of the car then rushed inside of the hospital. We went to the emergency room where there was a crowd of people. I looked around until I spotted Lauren, Tori, and McKenzie's mother with a man that I didn't know.

I spoke to everyone before sitting down. Everyone spoke back except for the man. All he did was look me up and down. I didn't know his ass and now wasn't the time, so I ignored him.

"What was that about? Who is buddy?" Josh whispered.

"Man, I don't know, just leave it alone until we find out what's going on," I replied.

"Oh my God, baby, I'm so glad you made it," Lauren cried as she jumped into Martez's arms.

"Calm down, baby, what happened? Where's my sister?" Martez asked.

"They took her to the back to check on her and get an x-ray done. She was unconscious when we got here. Tori and I got our vitals checked in the ambulance and were fine, so we didn't have to go in the emergency room. I tried to call you, but my phone died," Lauren rattled on.

"Alright, my dad is on his way here. He's bringing Keena with him. He's going to call when he's outside and you're going to have to go back to the house with her. I promise I will keep you updated, and I'll come back to the house with you as soon as possible," Martez assured her.

Once their conversation was over, I decided to speak up.

"Can one of y'all tell me what happened? I know it was a car accident, but how did y'all crash?" I asked.

I needed to know exactly what happened. With the life-style we lived, we couldn't be too careful. I wanted to make sure it was an accident and no one ran them off the road.

Tori looked at McKenzie's mom and then turned her attention to Lauren. She looked like she was battling whether to tell us what happened or not. She opened her mouth to speak but stopped when Tyrese, Quan, and Tino entered the room.

"What the hell happened? Where are Niyah, Kenzie, and Charmaine?" Tyrese yelled.

"Boy, sit down with all that yelling before you get us kicked out this hospital. It's already more of us here than should be. They're all in the back getting checked up," McKenzie's mother, Celeste, stated.

"Okay, what happened though? Who was driving?" Tyrese asked again.

"The accident was Aniyah's fault. She's the one that was driving. She was too busy arguing and texting with Quan to pay attention to the road. Charmaine offered to drive instead and Kenzie asked to get out of the car, but she didn't listen. She was in the middle of a text and the light turned red. Instead of trying to reverse, she went for the text and someone ran into the car. It spun out of control and we ran into a parked car. Luckily we all had seat belts on or it could've been worse.

Kenzie was sitting in the back on the side that was hit, and I think she hit her head against the window and I know her leg was stuck. They had to cut that side of the car out. Charmaine hit her head, but I'm not sure what other injuries, and Aniyah's head hit the steering wheel as well, but the air bag came out," Lauren explained.

"How the fuck you gone blame the accident on my sister and she's injured while you sitting out here fine?" Tyrese shouted.

"Yo, who the fuck you talking to? If the accident was Aniyah's fault, it was hers. Don't nobody got to sugar coat shit for the sake of your feelings," Martez bellowed as he jumped in Tyrese's face.

"What are you trying to do though, Tez? You know we don't even rock like this, but we can if you want to."

"Shut your bitch ass up, you ain't rocking with shit. McKenzie talks to me about everything, so I already know how you get down."

"That's enough, you two need to take a breather," the man I didn't know said as he stood between them.

"Ricky, if you don't get the fuck out of my face, I'll lay your ass out on this floor. You already know I don't fuck with your ass after what you did to my sister," Tez said.

Now I knew who the guy was. McKenzie told me all about her stepfather, but I had never seen him before.

"Come on, Ricky, sit down," Celeste begged.

"Yeah, listen to your wife and sit your ass down before you get knocked out. The only reason I ain't did it yet is because McKenzie told me to leave it alone."

Ricky did as he was told and sat down by his wife while Tez and Tyrese continued to give each other death stares.

"Did someone call my brother?" Tino asked.

"I tried calling a couple times from Kenzie's phone before it died," Tori answered.

I shook my head and sat back in my seat. Of course, that nigga didn't answer his calls. Even though I wasn't in the picture when she was fucking with him, I hated she was having kids by that dumb ass nigga. He didn't deserve to be with her and he definitely didn't deserve for her to carry his kids.

"Hello, I'm Dr. Chin, are you all the family of Charmaine Watson, Aniyah Watson, and McKenzie Alvarez?"

"Yes, Doctor, how are they doing?" Celeste questioned.

"Aniyah has a bump on her head and sprained wrist. Other than that she's fine and will be released shortly. Charmaine is on her way to surgery right now. Her right arm and leg are broken and she has some cracked ribs. As for McKenzie, we moved her upstairs to labor and delivery. We did an x-ray and nothing is broken. Her ankle and leg are severely swollen and she has a minor concussion. We did an ultrasound and the babies are fine right now. However, due to the pain she's in, it's causing her blood pressure to rise. We can't do much to relieve her pain while the kids are inside. We feel that an emergency cesarean is needed so we can help her and make sure the kids don't go into distress," Dr. Chin advised us.

"What floor is labor and delivery? I need to go see my sister before you all do anything," Martez said.

"It's on the fifth floor, she's in room 539. There's a waiting room up there as well."

"Alright, thank you," Martez replied before his phone started to ring. He answered it then grabbed Lauren's hand, so I assumed that it was his father.

Me, Tori, Josh, and Tino got on the elevator and headed upstairs while everyone else stayed in the emergency room. I was surprised that McKenzie's mother didn't come up as well.

I'm hoping that she's waiting on Aniyah to be released then coming up to see about her other daughter.

When we made it upstairs, Josh and Tino stayed in the waiting room while me and Tori went to McKenzie's room. My heart broke when I saw McKenzie laying there looking pale. I wished I could take all of her pain away. There was a machine attached to her stomach and an IV hooked up to her arm. It looked like they were also giving her oxygen.

"Hey, what is your relationship to Ms. Alvarez?" the nurse asked.

"I'm her boyfriend," I lied.

"Okay, I'm not sure what the doctor told you, but right now we've given her a couple shots of steroids to help strengthen the twins' lungs. She's also sedated to help relieve some of the pain. We were trying to hold out a bit longer before doing the cesarean, but her blood pressure isn't going down so we're prepping a room now. You won't be able to go in with her, but you can wait the waiting room and then meet her in recovery. Once the procedure is done she'll be moved upstairs and we'll have to take the twins to the NICU to run some tests since they are coming six weeks early."

"Alright, can you just wait a couple minutes before taking her? Her father and brother are on their way up the stairs right now."

As soon as those words left my mouth, Tez and his dad came rushing in the room. I told them what the nurse said then they walked over to McKenzie. I stepped out of the room so they could have some privacy with her. I sat down in a chair and Tori sat down next to me.

"Do you need anything?" she asked.

"You were the one that was just in an accident. I should be asking you that," I chuckled.

"I know, but I can tell that you're worried about McKenzie. She's strong and she's going to pull through this."

I nodded my head then leaned back against the wall.

"They're taking her to do the c-section now. Someone should be contacting us in about an hour with an update," Martez announced.

"McKenzie is going to wake up and not feel those kids in her stomach and have a fit. You know she had everything planned out," I said.

"Man, tell me about it," Martez mumbled.

We all sat around and talked while Tino kept calling Chase over and over without getting an answer. After a while, he gave up and put his phone in his pocket.

An hour and fifteen minutes went by before a doctor came into the room.

"Hello, I'm Doctor Jensen. I performed the cesarean on Ms. Alvarez. Twin A, which is a boy, weighs 5 lbs 3 oz and is 17 inches. Twin B, which is a girl, weighs 4 lbs 9 oz and is 16.5 inches. They're both breathing on their own, but we still have to run some tests on them. If all goes well, they should be released within the next couple days. Ms. Alverez is still in recovery but should be moved to a room within the next thirty minutes. Do not be alarmed, but she will still be under heavy sedation. We want to leave her like that for a few more hours due to heavy bleeding during the procedure. We believe it was due to her hitting her stomach during the accident. We gave her a blood transfusion and we expect her to have a full recovery. She's going to be moved to room 625, and it is a private suite per your request, Mr. Alvarez. Three of you can go in to see her at a time, but only one will be permitted to stay overnight."

"Thank you, Dr. Jensen," said Victor.

"I'm glad she's going to be alright. I'm going to head out

now. Nita and I will come back up here tomorrow to check on her. If you need anything, give me a call," Josh stated.

"Thank you, I appreciate you staying. I'll make sure to let Kenz know."

I dapped Josh up and hugged Nita before they left. The rest of us went upstairs. Me, Martez, and Victor waited in McKenzie's room while Tori and Tino went to the waiting room.

I stood staring out of the window at all of the hustle and bustle that was going on outside. Like clockwork, they brought McKenzie in thirty minutes later. It felt like I could finally breathe again when I laid eyes on her. I know the doctors said she was okay, but it was like I needed to see it myself. I pulled a chair over to McKenzie's bed and held her hand while Victor and Martez sat in the couch across the room. From what I could hear, they were updating their family on McKenzie's condition.

"Is anyone allowed to see the babies?" I asked the nurse.

"Yes, both parents and grandparents are allowed. However, we have to wait for Mom to be stable before anyone can actually go in and see them because paperwork needs to be filled out. I can make an exception and take one of you down now to see them and you can take some pictures, but you won't be able to touch them."

"Okay, I'll wait here. You can let her brother or father go down," I suggested.

"I'll go down, Pops don't know nothing about taking pictures," Martez laughed. For the first time since we'd been here, he finally relaxed as well. I guess we were both just waiting to make sure everything was fine with McKenzie.

"Boy, don't act like I'm old. I'll hit your ass upside your head. You go, though, I need to go to the waiting room to talk to Celeste because I don't like the fact that she ain't found her way to our daughter's room yet," Victor said seriously.

Victor and Martez left the room, leaving me alone with McKenzie. I rubbed the bandage that was on her forehead and kissed her on the cheek softly.

"I'm so damn glad that you're alright. I don't know what I would have done if you didn't pull through. You're going to get strong, and I'm going to take you on a proper date in a couple months when you're up to it. I don't know if you know this, but I'm kind of falling for you," I whispered in her ear.

I wasn't sure if McKenzie could hear me, but it felt good to get that off of my chest.

CHAPTER NINE

CHASE

I fumbled with my keys trying to open my front door. I was tipsy and high as hell. My mama would kick my ass if she knew I drove all the way home like this. I had the window down and my music blasting to keep me alert the entire time. After trying a couple more times, I finally got the door open.

I walked in the house and Diane was laying on the couch watching TV in a pair of boy shorts and a tank top. The one day I decided to come in early, she would be sitting down here on the couch looking good as hell.

"Hey, you actually came back home the same day you left out," she said sarcastically.

"Yeah, I finished work and didn't feel like hanging out." I shrugged before walking past her and into the kitchen.

I looked in the microwave and saw Diane had a plate for me like always. I warmed up the food then sat down at the table to eat. She had cooked tilapia, spaghetti, corn on the cob, and rolls. I had the munchies so I dove right in, eating my food within ten minutes. I washed it down with a Sprite.

"Damn, you was hungry, you ate that fast as hell. None of your bitches fed you today?" Diane asked from the doorway.

"You just did," I said sarcastically.

"Don't play with me, Chase. I'm not your bitch or your woman. If I was, we would be sleeping in the same bed every night and you wouldn't be letting the sun beat you home. If I was, it wouldn't have been months since the last time we made love," Diane replied, on the verge of tears.

"I'm sorry, you're right. You're not my bitch, but neither is anybody else."

"What about McKenzie?" she countered.

"What about her? I told you that nothing is going on between me and that girl. We barely even talk unless it has to do with the babies."

"Then why aren't we sleeping in the same bed, Chase? I know you love sex, so you're not going to make me believe you not out there fucking nobody."

"It's not even like that, Diane. I told you I wasn't taking a break because of McKenzie. I wanted the break to give you time to think," I reminded her.

"I have been thinking and I'm tired of thinking. That's all I do every night when I go to bed alone and wonder about who you're laying up with."

"That's the problem then, you're thinking about the wrong shit. I'm not laying up with nobody every night. You're supposed to be thinking about whether you can accept my kids or not."

"I told you from the beginning I can, Chase."

"Okay, bet, they'll be here soon then we'll revisit this conversation," I told her before walking away.

I walked upstairs and went to the bathroom across from my room. I turned on the shower to allow the water to get hot while I brushed my teeth. Once I was done, I climbed in the shower and allowed the hot water to run over my body, hoping it would sober me up.

I honestly don't know what the hell is going on with me, but I need to get a grip on my life before someone catches me slipping. I've always been a smoker but I never got drunk every day. Ever since I saw McKenzie with that nigga Blaze at her house, I've been drinking every day until the point where I'm ready to pass out, and that's not a good look. It's like I hit a self-destruction button when this shit went down. Then, to make matters worse, she had him at our kids' baby shower. I kept quiet and my distance there because I wanted to peep everything that was going on. From what I could tell, her family liked him because they were engaged with him most of the evening when she wasn't. I really wanted to know how long had she known him for them all to seem so close. I couldn't ask now, though, without the risk of her cursing me out.

I'm not going to lie. When I saw them smiling and looking happy at her shower, I felt like an outsider. As much as I wanted to stay mad at dude for sliding in on Kenzie, I couldn't because I brought this shit on myself. McKenzie's a beautiful woman, pregnant and all, so there was no way I should have expected her to just wait around for me to figure my shit out. If it wasn't Blaze, it'd be another man standing there ready to wife Kenz and play stepdaddy to my kids. It's the aura and the vibe that she gives off. Once you get to know her, you can't help but fall for her no matter the circumstances.

I know people don't believe me when I say it and Kenzie probably doesn't either, but I really do love that damn girl. I just wasn't mature enough at the time to realize what was right in front of me. I should've ended things with Diane before I had sex with Kenzie. I knew long before Kenzie and I had sex that I wanted to be with her. That was the time when I should have been sitting down with Diane and explaining to her that I wasn't feeling our relationship anymore. Long before she even moved into my house or found out Kenzie was pregnant.

I finished showering and dried off then walked back into my bedroom where Diane was lying in bed naked.

"What are you doing in here, D?" I asked.

"I want to spend the night with you. Just for tonight, then we can go back to sleeping in different rooms. Please, I miss you and need you to make love to me," she begged.

I thought about it for a minute, and it went against my better judgment, but I climbed into bed and got under the covers with her. I stared at the ceiling deep in thought, battling with wrong from right. After laying there for a few minutes in silence, I decided to break it.

"I'm not sure this is a good idea. I'm not trying to confuse you and make matters worse," I admitted.

"Why don't you want me anymore? What is it about that little ass girl? I know it's not the looks because I'm pretty too, and my ass, breasts, and thighs are bigger than hers. Does she suck your dick or enjoy you eating her out? If that's what it is, we can fix this now," Diane said.

"This has nothing to do with McKenzie, so please stop bringing her up in every conversation we have. I wasn't with her for one reason, and the reasons I was had nothing to do with me and you," I told her as nicely as possibly.

"Okay, well let's change one of those reasons," she stated.

I was wondering what she was talking about until she got under the covers and placed my manhood in her mouth. Part of me wanted to protest, but the other part needed the release so I laid back and let her do her thing.

The head was trash, but I didn't want to hurt her feelings since she was making an effort.

After five minutes of her choking, I decided to put her out of her misery and flipped her over.

I kissed her lips then trailed kisses down her body until I made it to her pussy. I dipped my tongue in and started sucking on her clit. I was barely there for a minute and she was pushing me away already. I tried to keep going, but she was choking the shit out of me with her thighs, so I gave up and grabbed a condom from the nightstand drawer.

Diane claimed she was on birth control again but as far as I knew, after she found out Kenzie was pregnant, she could've went and got off that shit. I couldn't afford any chances right now, especially with the twins on the way. I was already about to be stretched thin with them. I wouldn't know what to do with three kids right now.

I opened the condom wrapper and put the condom on before sliding inside of Diane gently. A moan escaped both of our mouths because her shit was tight as hell as it gripped my dick. I leaned down and bit her shoulder blade gently as I picked up the pace some.

"Damn, D, you missed this dick, baby?" I asked as I gave her nothing but deep strokes.

"Yesss, Chase, just like that, baby. I'm about to cum," she cried out.

Diane's body convulsed as she came all over my dick. I flipped her over and rammed my dick in from the back. She threw her ass back as I put in work on that pussy. Surprisingly, Diane didn't complain about the pace of how fast I was going. If she wasn't going to say anything, then I wasn't going to stop until I got my nut off. I did know that she didn't like long rounds, and I didn't want to torture her further than I already had, so after a few more minutes I was ready to cum.

"I'm about to nut," I groaned as I pulled the condom off and nutted on her back.

Diane jumped up from the bed and walked out of the room to the bathroom, I assumed so she could get cleaned up. I had just fucked her the same way I've been doing Bri the last couple days, minus the eating pussy part. I wouldn't dare eat Bri out because she's not my woman, and I know for a fact she's fucking other niggas. The only thing different here is I didn't jump up and take money from my wallet for Diane.

Diane came in the room ten minutes later with a towel wrapped around her body and a small one. She used the small one to clean me off before climbing in the bed. Out of habit, I pulled her close to me and wrapped my arms around her body.

"I really want us to work, Chase, but I need you to meet me halfway," Diane said.

I didn't know what to tell her and I didn't want to give out false hope, so instead of replying I pulled her closer to me.

It was only 9 p.m. but I was tired as hell, so I closed my eyes and went to sleep.

I woke up a couple hours later with the urge to use the bathroom. I got up and released my bladder then went back to my bedroom. I searched for my phone because it wasn't on the nightstand where I put it anymore.

I looked for my phone for about five minutes before I gave up and went to shake Diane awake.

"Diane, do you know where my phone is?" I asked.

"No, why would I know where it is?" she countered.

"Come on now with the goofy shit. I left my phone on the nightstand and unless Casper lives here, my shit should be where I left it."

Diane mumbled some shit under her voice then stormed out of the bedroom. About a minute later, she returned with my phone on silent.

"Here, your bitch and brother been calling you," she said as she handed me my phone.

I snatched it from her and looked through the call log. I had calls from McKenzie, Quan, and Tino.

I tried calling Kenzie first, but her phone was going straight to voicemail, so I called Tino next.

"Man, what the fuck, we've been trying to reach your ass for hours," Tino yelled all in one breath. If Tino was acting like this, I knew something was wrong.

"My bad, bro, what's going on?"

"McKenzie was in a car accident. They had to give her a c-section to deliver the twins.

"Fuck, what hospital is she at?"

"Rush Oak Park, I'm still up here but I haven't seen her."

"Alright, I'm getting dressed now." I hung up the phone and grabbed a pair of boxers, joggers, and a t-shirt. I got dressed as fast as possible.

"Is everything alright?" Diane asked.

"No, it's not. Don't fucking silence or touch my phone again. You trying to be on some slick shit when the calls that were coming through were important."

"I'm sorry, Chase, I didn't know."

"Of course, you didn't know, and you didn't care. I told you that McKenzie don't fuck with me like that, so if she's calling me it has something to do with our kids. You say you're going to be there and accept my kids, but then you go and pull some shit like this," I yelled.

"What can I do to fix this?" Diane asked.

"Nothing, I have to go. I'll call to you later," I told her before walking out of the room. I grabbed my keys and put on my coat then was out of the house. I sped the entire drive to the hospital, hoping that Kenzie and our kids were fine. I just know she's going to curse me out for not answering her calls. This is the one thing I was trying to prove to her wouldn't be a problem.

I found a park in the garage then walked over to the hospital. I gave the lady at the desk McKenzie's name, and she gave me her room number. When I got in the elevator, I pressed the number six for mother and baby unit then said a silent prayer. I wasn't much of a religious person, but I needed to believe that someone was up there looking down on us, because I didn't know what I was about to walk in on.

When I got off the elevator, I walked past the waiting room and saw some of McKenzie's family and Tino.

"Hey man, you made it," Tino said.

"Yeah, Diane's dumb ass silenced and hid my phone."

"Did you see Kenzie yet?"

"Nah, I was on my way there but saw y'all here. What happened?"

"All I know is Aniyah and Quan got into it. Aniyah wasn't paying attention while driving and somebody ran into them."

"Where is Aniyah?"

"She's downstairs with her father and uncle. Charmaine had surgery and has to stay overnight."

I nodded my head in understanding then walked away. I pushed the door open to McKenzie's room and saw her father, Tez, and Blaze in the room. Her father and brother were sitting on a couch across from her bed while Blaze was in a recliner with his eyes closed. I couldn't tell if he was asleep or not.

I looked at McKenzie and there was an IV hooked in. One was filled with blood and there were a few other ones with clear liquid, which I assumed was some kind of medication. Her right leg was bandaged and elevated some.

"Look who finally decided to show up," Martez said, looking up at me.

"My bad, my phone was on silent, and I didn't know it. How is she doing?" I asked.

"She's fine, she had the twins about three hours ago. They have her sedated so they can stabilize the pain and her blood pressure. They're going to start weening her off of it soon. Both babies are breathing on their own and seem to be doing good as well. They're in NICU for observation," McKenzie's father said.

"Okay, thank you. What are you doing here? Did you watch my kids be born?" I asked Blaze, whose eyes were now open and looking at me.

"Dude, why the fuck are you talking to me? McKenzie's been here for almost five hours and you're just now getting here, but you're worried about why I'm here? Worry about how it only took one call for me to be here by her bedside and you're just strolling in like shit's good."

"Nigga—" I started but was cut off by Victor.

"Listen here, I don't know what the hell is going on between you two and frankly, I don't give a damn. My daughter is laying up here in a hospital bed in pain, and that's something none of us has control over. She doesn't need to wake up to this bullshit. Chase, you might not want Blaze here but McKenzie does, so he's not going anywhere. He was the one that was there to pick up the pieces that you broke, so he stays. You can either deal with it or leave," he said calmly but with authority.

McKenzie's father was a man that demanded respect without having to ask for it. It was just something about his demeanor. Kenzie never told me much about her father and brother. All she said was they were businessmen, but I knew it was more than that. I couldn't stand being in there with Blaze and his cocky ass, so I walked out of the room and went to the waiting room. I'd go back in once McKenzie was woke to see her.

CHAPTER TEN

MCKENZIE

It's amazing how your life could change in the blink of an eye. Today started off great and all it took was a nigga to knock my sister off her square for things to turn bad. All I remember is one minute I'm arguing with Aniyah and the next thing someone's crashing into us.

I've been struggling to open my eyes for God knows how long, but it feels like they're glued shut. I would say I'm dead, but I know that's not true from the amount of pain my body is in. I could hear everything around me, but I was unable to respond. I don't know what the hell is going on, but I don't like it one bit. Something feels off and I can't put my finger on it. If only I could open my eyes, then I can see for myself.

After trying to open my eyes for what felt like an eternity, I finally succeeded.

I turned my head to the left and saw Malakai sitting in a chair next to me asleep. I could hear machines beeping in my ear, so I turned my head to the right and saw the machine hooked up to me indicating that I was in the hospital.

I lifted my arm up and looked at the IV in my arm. Tears

welled up in my eyes from the pain I was feeling. I had never felt such pain in my nineteen years of life. It was like my entire body was hurting from my head down to my toes, which I was barely able to move.

I put my hand on my stomach and it was no longer hard. It had actually gone down some, and that's when I started to panic and hyperventilate. I just knew I had lost my kids in that accident. If that was true, I don't think I'll ever be able to forgive Aniyah for this shit.

I opened my mouth to talk but it was dry as hell. The more I panicked, the machines started beeping causing Malakai to finally wake up.

"Shhhh, ma, calm down," Malakai said as he rubbed the side of my face.

I don't know how he could want me to calm down in a situation like this. Even if I knew how to calm down, I couldn't.

"What happened?" some nurse asked as she rushed in my room with a doctor.

"I don't know, she just woke up," Malakai answered.

"Should we sedate her again?" the nurse asked the doctor.

"No, don't give my daughter any more of that shit. Just give us a minute with her and we can calm her down. You've been drugging her for almost forty-eight hours," my father said as he walked in the room with my brother and Chase.

Forty-eight hours? I've been out of it for almost two days? What the hell, I thought to myself.

"Princesa, I need you to relax and then we can explain everything to you. If you don't, they're going to give you drugs to go back to sleep again," my father explained calmly as he rubbed the top of my head.

I willed myself to calm down and my breathing slowly but surely got back to normal. I didn't want to sleep anymore because I needed to know what was going on. More importantly, I needed to know what happened to my kids.

"I need water," I whispered. I hope the water will take this harsh feeling away from my throat.

The nurse left out of the room and returned with some ice chips. I know I asked for some damn water, but I guess I'll take what I can get.

I sucked on some of the ice chips and they helped soothe my throat.

"Hi, Ms. Alvarez, my name is Dr. Jensen. How are you feeling?" the doctor asked.

"Like I've been hit by a truck. Did I lose my twins?" I asked afraid of the answer.

"Oh no, both of your babies are healthy and doing good. You were brought in here Saturday evening due to a car accident. Your leg and ankle were severely swollen and you had a concussion. Your blood pressure was high and we did everything we could to try and slow down labor, but we ended up having to give you a cesarean. You've been sedated most of the time you were here. We tried taking the sedation off you, but each time your blood pressure was still out of control due to the pain your body was in. We've been giving you medication to help with the inflammation and we also had to give you a blood transfusion. Now that you're awake, we can give you a morphine drip if you want. We'd like to keep you in here for the next three days to make sure your cesarean scar is healing well," Dr. Jensen explained.

"Okay, when can I see my kids?"

"Let me examine you and I'll have a nurse take you down a wheelchair. You can only stay for a few minutes, though, then you need to get back to bed."

"Alright, thank you."

"Gentlemen, I need you all to step out while I perform the

exam. You can come back in about ten minutes," Dr. Jensen requested.

They all turned to leave out including Malakai, but I didn't want to be alone so I grabbed his arm before he could leave out of the room.

"Can you please stay?" I asked.

"Of course," he replied as he sat back in the seat.

Chase gave me a look of death, but I didn't care. I needed him to know I was serious about not fucking with him like that anymore. If I really wanted to give Malakai a shot, I needed to show him that he came before Chase.

"How long have you been here?" I questioned as the doctor started my exam.

"I've been here ever since you got here. Josh brought me a change of clothes and some food yesterday when he and Nita came to see you. They said they'll be back again today. Your father and brother kept trying to get me to go home and get some rest, but I needed to be here when you woke up so I could know for myself that you're alright."

"Thank you, I appreciate that." I smiled.

"You're welcome, you should know by now that I'll do anything for you," he said sincerely.

"Oh, he's a keeper," Dr. Jensen added.

I couldn't help but smile at her comment. She was definitely right about that. Malakai was not only fine but caring and gentle when it came to me, but I also knew he was a beast in the streets, so that meant he could protect me. I'd be a damn fool not to give him a chance. I knew from the beginning that he wasn't Chris or Chase. I can't penalize him for my former relationships.

"Am I able to take a shower?"

Right now you have a catheter inside of you but once the

nurse removes it you can, as long as you have someone to help you."

"Okay, thank you," I replied.

Once Dr. Jensen left the room, my father, Chase, Nita, Josh, and Martez came into the room. I was kind of disappointed that none of my other family or friends were here to see me.

"Oh my God, I'm so glad you're okay. I came to see you twice but you were out of it," Nita beamed as she ran over and hugged me.

"Thank you, Malakai told me that you and Josh had been here."

"Yeah, we tried to get him to leave with us but he wouldn't leave your bedside," Nita said

"He told me, and I'm glad you two came by. If it's not too much to ask, are you able to help me freshen up when my nurse comes back?"

"Of course, do you need me to go get anything for you?"

"I don't think so, my brother brought everything I need already."

"Mi hija, what do you want to eat? Lauren's going to come up here and I'm going to go home with McKenna. Lauren and Tori have been taking turns coming up here to see you. Tori had to go back to work today, but she said she'll be up here tomorrow during visiting hours. Your mother and siblings were up here earlier but they left. I called your mother and told her you were up, so she said she'd come back up here later as well."

"Some soup from Panera will good."

"Okay, I love you," my father told me.

"I love you too, Papa."

"I'm about to get out of here too and go home to help Pops with Kenna. We'll be back up here tomorrow to see. I'm sure you'll be in good hands," Martez stated knowingly, looking over at Malakai.

"Hey, the NICU said there's some paperwork that you need to fill out so I'm able to go in with the kids. The people also came around for us to do the paperwork for the social security cards and birth certificates," Chase said, speaking up for the first time since he's been in my room.

"Hey, okay, when my nurse comes in I'll ask her to call for the people. I'm sure once I go down you can go with me."

"Okay, I'm going to go sit on the couch if that's cool with you," Chase said

"Yeah, it's fine."

A couple minutes after that, my nurse came in the room to take the catheter out.

"Come on, bro, your girl woke now and you see that she's good. Let's go grab something to eat while the nurse and Nita do what they need to do," Josh suggested.

I expected Malakai to correct Josh for calling me his girlfriend, but all he did was smirk before getting up from his seat. He leaned over and kissed me on the forehead.

"Do you need anything before I leave?"

"You can get me some fruit depending on where you're going."

"I don't know where we're going, but we can stop somewhere to get the fruit for you on the way back," Malakai stated before walking out of the room.

The nurse removed my catheter and I sat up in the bed. My body ached like crazy, but I needed to get out of the bed. Nita helped me up and we went into the bathroom. She turned the shower on for me and helped me out of my gown. I took the pad off that someone put on for me and trashed it along with the hospital panties.

"Uhm, you can sit on the toilet if you want. I don't want you to feel uncomfortable seeing me naked."

"Girl bye, if you don't get your ass in that shower. I'll be right there with you because if you fall or something happens, I won't hear the end of it from Blaze, and those beautiful babies of yours need their mother in good health."

I pulled the shower chair up under the water and sat in it. The water cascading over my body felt good as hell. It didn't take away all the pain, but it helped ease it a lot. I held my head under the water and closed my eyes. I stayed there for a good ten minutes before actually washing up with my Dove body wash. I scrubbed my body until I felt clean again.

Once I was done, I got up and dried off. Nita handed me a pair of underwear and a sanitary napkin from the bag. I put that on with a tank top, t-shirt, and socks. I know that Lauren had to have helped Martez pack this bag, because there was no way Martez would have remembered to put all of this, especially the pads. I brushed my teeth and I was feeling like a million bucks.

Nita grabbed my bag and we went back in the bedroom where Martez was sitting doing something on his phone.

"Do you mind sitting here while we go see the kids? Lauren should be here in a little while and they're only allowing me to go for thirty minutes, so I might as well go now."

"Go ahead, I'll sit here and watch TV. I know you are anxious to see your babies."

"Okay, thank you so much." I smiled.

I buzzed for the nurse, and she called for transportation. After waiting for almost ten minutes, they showed up with a wheelchair. They wheeled me down to the elevator and we took it down to the fourth floor.

When we made it in the NICU and I saw my twins, my

heart melted. They were so damn beautiful. I couldn't believe they were a part of me.

"Hey Mom, do we have names for your babies?" the nurse asked.

"Yes, my daughter is Chance Alexandria James-Alvarez, and my son is Chase Alexander James-Alvarez," I said.

Chase wanted the kids to have his name, but I felt like I needed to hyphenate it with my last name as well. Chase claimed he'll always be there for our kids, but I don't know. He's not too happy with Malakai in the picture, so there's no telling if he's going to back away from his responsibilities. I didn't want my kids having the last name of someone who won't be in their lives.

We stayed in the NICU for the thirty minutes then went back up to my room where Lauren, Nita, Josh, and Malakai were sitting down talking. Chase stood in the corner of the room being anti-social. He didn't say anything to anyone, so they didn't say anything to him. Once the case manager came back with the paperwork, we both signed and filled it out, then he left to go about his business.

Everyone sat around and talked until visiting hours were over, then they left as well, leaving me and Malakai alone. I don't know what's wrong with me, but I'm feeling nervous as hell. I've never been nervous about saying what's on my mind to anyone, including Malakai.

"Are you alright?" Malakai asked. His voice was filled with concern. Now I felt bad for making him worry.

"Yes, I'm okay. Uhm, I just wanted to talk to you about something."

"Okay, what's up?"

"I just want to say I appreciate everything that you have been doing for me and how patient you have been. You being here this entire time and me having that accident is a wake-up call. I'm ready, I don't want to wait any longer for us to be together. That's if you're ready to give up all your girls and only be with me, because the only people I'm willing to share you with are Marquis and Makayla."

"Shut up, I told you I'm ready when you are. All you had to do was say the word," Malakai said before leaning over and kissing me gently on the lips. I held the back of his head and deepened the kiss. His lips felt just as good as I thought they would. I had to break the kiss and remind myself that I just had twins. I could already tell I was going to be in trouble fucking with Malakai, because as soon as I feel comfortable and snap back, I was going to bust it wide open for this man.

Malakai and I sat back and talked for a couple of hours about any and everything. I could tell that he was tired, but he wasn't going to fall asleep before me. It was the same way whenever we were at my house. He always waited for me to fall asleep before he closed his eyes.

CHAPTER ELEVEN
ANIYAH

I stood in my room pacing back and forth, not sure what to do. I needed to go see McKenzie but the truth is, I'm scared to face her. How do I look my sister in the eyes knowing I was the cause of her going into labor early? My mother told me she's doing fine and so are the babies, but it's the principle of things. I was reckless with not only my life but everyone else in the car as well.

The accident could be so much worse than it was. Charmaine isn't even answering my calls right now. My uncle Craig and my father told me to just give her some time. Plus, the medication they gave her to take home is making her sleep a lot. It's crazy how I was the cause of the accident but Charmaine and McKenzie got the short end of the stick.

Quan had been blowing me up ever since the accident, talking about come see the surprise he has for me. I'm tired of sitting in the house and I have no car, so I told him he could come pick me up. His surprise better be good if he wants me to forgive him for what he did. I still can't believe out of all the bitches he could cheat on me with, he chose my stepsister.

My phone went off and I looked at It, seeing that it was Quan letting me know he was outside. I grabbed my phone and purse then headed to the front. I put my coat on then walked outside to Quan's car.

"Hey baby, I'm glad you finally agreed to meet up with me. I've been going crazy not being able to see or talk to you."

"Well nigga, you should've thought about that before you decided to fuck another bitch."

"I know, I told you that it was a mistake. Shavon don't mean shit to me."

"Apparently, I don't mean shit to you either," I mumbled.

The rest of the car ride was quiet. We drove for about twenty-five minutes until we pulled up to a house in Bellwood. I had no idea whose house it was and I didn't care. I know he didn't find a new person's house for us to fuck at.

"Come on, let's get out," Quan said.

I got out of the car and followed Quan to the house. He used a key to open the door and we stepped in. He gave me a tour of the house and it was nice. It had three bedrooms with a basement and attic. It was already fully furnished minus one of the bedrooms.

"What are we doing here, Quan?"

"This is part of the surprise I have for you. This is the house I promised you. You can finally move out of your mother's house and in with me."

I had mixed emotions hearing those words from Quan. I wanted this for two years, but now I don't know how to feel after everything happened. I mean, he must be serious about me if he went out and got us a house.

"Okay, what's the other surprise?" I asked, trying not to show any excitement.

"I wanted to do this different but you weren't talking to me. I love you, Aniyah, and I want to spend the rest of my life with you. Will you marry me?" Quan asked as he pulled a small velvet box from his pocket. He opened it and there was a 1-ct, princess diamond-cut ring in it. The ring wasn't flashy, but it was still beautiful to me.

"Yes, Quan, I'll marry you, baby. I love you and all is forgiven, just don't let it happen again," I warned him.

"It won't. Now do you want to go out and have dinner, or do you want to order take out?"

"I'd rather make love to my fiancé and figure dinner out later," I purred.

"Well, we can definitely arrange that." Quan smiled.

Quan and I stripped out of our clothes then made love all over the house. His stroke game didn't seem to be a problem tonight. I don't if it was because we had the house to ourselves so we were free to do whatever we wanted. Whatever it was, I enjoyed it and hoped that it was always like this.

Once we finished making love, Quan and I laid in our bed and cuddled together.

"How is your sister?" Quan asked.

"I haven't talked to her yet. My mother told me she woke up yesterday, but I've been scared to talk to her. I'm going to go see her tomorrow, though, for sure. I don't want her to feel like I abandoned her after the accident."

"Yeah, you need to talk to her. Your sister is a very under-standing person. Go see her and make things right with her."

"I will, but enough about that. When do you want to get married?"

"I was thinking we can go to Vegas in a couple of weeks and elope. I just bought this house, so I don't think we should be spending a lot on a wedding and honeymoon. We can do it this way now and then next year on our wedding anniversary, we can have a real wedding and reception."

"That sounds perfect, I don't need a big wedding. I'll just

be happy to have your last name and then we can work on having babies. We can do things the right way."

"I like the sound of that. I'm about to order us something to eat. You just lay here and relax," Quan said before leaving out of the room to go get his phone.

I laid in bed staring at my beautiful diamond ring. I couldn't wait to tell everybody I was engaged. I finally had something that McKenzie didn't have, and it felt amazing. For once in our lives, I wasn't the fuck up in the family. I was moving out of my mother's house and into my own. Granted, Quan and I's relationship wasn't perfect, but whose was?

I climbed out of bed and walked into the ensuite bathroom. I brushed my teeth then took a shower. It felt good to finally have a place of my own. I didn't have anyone to answer to anymore. I don't have to tell my mother my whereabouts or find somebody's house or the trap to go to when I want to have sex with my man. I can just roll over and jump on his dick whenever I wanted.

I finished up my shower and wrapped a towel around me then went back in the bedroom. I wanted to call and check on McKenzie, so I went back downstairs and grabbed my phone. It rang four times before she finally picked up.

"Hello," she answered groggily.

"Hey, I'm sorry, did I wake you?"

"Yeah, but it's fine. These meds they have me on keep me sluggish," she replied.

"I just wanted to call and tell you how sorry I am. If I could change things, I would do it all so differently."

"It's alright, I'm okay and so are the twins. We have to stay here two more days but then we can go home."

"That's good, I'm so glad to hear that. Quan and I are getting married. I wanted you to be the first person to know," I beamed.

The phone line was silent for a minute before she finally said something.

"Are you serious? He proposed and you said yes?" McKenzie asked, confused.

"Of course, I said yes, I love him. What else was I supposed to say?"

"You was supposed to say you needed time to think about the shit. I mean, you just found him fucking somebody else a few days ago. You don't find it odd that he wants to marry you all of a sudden?"

"No, it's not odd. He bought us a house too. All of us just can't say fuck our nigga and jump in the next man's bed because he fucked up, like you," I spat.

"Girl, I know you tried it. I don't jump from bed to bed so don't even play with me."

I was about to respond when a male voice came on the line.

"Aye, I don't know what's going on, but McKenzie is hanging up now. She's laid up in a hospital bed and you're looking for a fight with her? This not even how this about to go, shorty," he told me before hanging up.

I sighed and laid my phone down. I couldn't even get mad at him for coming to my sister's defense. I have no business picking a fight with her in the hospital, but she irks my nerves sometimes. I called her with my good news and she just brushed the shit off like it didn't mean anything.

I'm not about to let McKenzie or anyone else ruin my mood or make me feel bad about my engagement. I'm not going to tell anyone else about it. I'm going to go to Vegas and get married then come back and rub the shit in everybody's face that doubted me.

CHAPTER TWELVE

CHASE

It's been three months since McKenzie had the twins. It still amazes me that I'm a father. When I look at them, it's like nothing else in the world matters. I can't believe they are a part of me. They're the perfect blend of me and McKenzie. My son is starting to look like me, but he has McKenzie's eyes, hair, and complexion. My daughter, on the other hand, is a mini version of McKenzie. I already know I'm going to have my hands full with her. I never thought I could love a person as much as I love them. I will protect them with my life no matter what.

"Baby, I was thinking we can go out tonight. It's been a while since we've been out on a date. We can go out to dinner and maybe a bar then come back home and make love," Diane suggested.

"I can't do dinner, but we can probably go to the bar," I replied.

"Why can't we go out to dinner? I'm tired of eating dinner by myself every night. You're barely fucking at home as it is. I think the least you could do is share a meal with me before you fuck me since that's all we do now anyway."

I sighed and sat on the edge of the bed.

"Come on now, Diane, it's not even like that. I've been working and spending time with my kids. I didn't get a chance to see them yesterday so I told McKenzie I'd be there today to spend some time with them."

"Why do you always have to go to her house? Why can't you bring the kids here? You know I won't do anything to them."

"I know that, baby, but this is what McKenzie and I agreed on until they're six months. She doesn't take them anywhere right now unless it's to a doctor's appointment. By then the summer will be here and she'll be more comfortable. I can't argue with her about that."

"Are you two back fucking?"

"Come on now, don't start this bullshit. I told you she doesn't want me. She has a new man now anyway and she's happy with him," I said.

Diane looked at me like she was debating on whether she believes me or not. I didn't give a fuck if she did; it was the truth.

Two weeks after McKenzie was released from the hospital, I went to her house to see the twins. I asked her if it was any chance that we can get back together. I told her I'd move out of the house with Diane and move back to my old place, but she wasn't having it. She told me she was with Blaze now, and all I could do was respect it. We set up a time frame for when I can see the kids and if I wanted to see them at a different time, I call and let her know.

I've run into Blaze a couple times when I've gone over to see my kids and we've kept it cordial. I'm not saying that we'll be friends, but I'll be respectful of McKenzie's house for the sake of my kids. As long as he's not doing anything to hurt her or the kids, I have to play my part because I don't want to do anything that'll piss McKenzie off to the point where I can't go there to see them.

Since McKenzie doesn't want me, I've slowly been falling back into my old ways. I'm back to sleeping in the same room with Diane. If I was a better man I'd still move out and allow Diane to stand on her own, but I just can't do it. I guess it has to do with me being comfortable and not wanting Diane to completely move on. I can't imagine Diane with another man when I'm the only one she's ever been with. When I do finally get my shit together, Diane will be the one I marry. I'm not trying to meet somebody and fall in love with them. With Diane, I already know what I'm getting.

"Okay, what time do you think you'll be back?" she finally asked.

"I'm not sure, probably around nine. Tino and Jennifer are meeting me at McKenzie's house to see the kids."

"So if nothing's going on between you two and your family is going over there, why can't I go as well to meet your kids? When we get married, I'm going to be their stepmother. Did you even ask McKenzie if it was okay for me to come with you one day?"

"No, I haven't, I'll talk to her about it though," I lied. I wasn't about to ask McKenzie could Diane come to her house. I didn't want Diane knowing where McKenzie lives at. The last thing I need is Diane popping up at McKenzie's house when I didn't show up at home. I was trying to put that off as long as I can.

"Alright, call me when you plan on leaving so I can be ready."

"I will, now just relax until I get home." I kissed Diane on the lips then grabbed my phone, keys, and wallet before heading out the house and driving to McKenzie's spot.

It took me twenty minutes to get to her house. When I pulled up I saw Tino's car in the driveway. He didn't even tell me he was here already. I grabbed the bags from the backseat with the formula and diapers for the twins. McKenzie breast feeds, but she also gives the kids formula because they be having her breasts hurting.

I rang McKenzie's doorbell and waited until Charmaine swung the door open.

"Hey Charmaine, what's going on?"

"Nothing much," she replied as she stepped out of the way to let me in.

I spoke to my brother and Jennifer then washed my hands before going to sit down next to them. They were both holding the twins, who were knocked out sleep.

"Where's Kenzie?" I asked.

"She had some errands to run but she'll be back in a little while," Charmaine answered.

"Cool, it's just you here?"

"Yeah, I've been here since yesterday. Tori went with McKenzie, so I stayed to watch the twins for her."

We all sat around and talked for about an hour until the back door opened and closed. Tori and McKenzie came in with shopping bags and sat them down on the island. McKenzie took her jacket off and washed her hands before walking over to us. I couldn't keep my eyes off of her. She looked good as hell, like she had just come back from the shop. Her makeup was done and her hair had fresh highlights with curls that flowed down her back. She was wearing a pair of blue Nike leggings with a half top that matched. The twins did McKenzie's body good. Her snap back game was no joke. You wouldn't be able to tell she had just had twins three months ago. Not to mention her breasts and ass were bigger now, giving her a grown woman body.

"Chase, are you going to keep staring at me or answer my question?" McKenzie asked, pulling me away from my thoughts.

"My bad, I didn't hear you. What did you ask?"

"I asked how long are you going to be here? I have plans so I'll be leaving at seven, but the twins will be here with Tori and Charmaine."

"Where are you going? I know you don't be leaving my kids already," I replied.

"Where I'm going is none of your business. I haven't been anywhere for the past three months. I have been couped up in this house long enough. The kids will be alright for a couple hours while I'm gone. Tori and Charmaine know where I'll be and the numbers to contact me in case of an emergency," Kenzie replied.

"Damn, it's like that now?" I countered.

"It's been like that. I'm not about to have this argument with you. I don't question you so you're not allowed to question me. You're here for the kids, not to be in my business."

"Okay, but I thought we could at least try to be friends."

"Alright, we can try this friend thing, but I'm still not telling you where I'm going." McKenzie smirked before getting up from the couch.

I watched McKenzie as she gathered the bags from the island and walked up the stairs.

"Jennifer, why don't you help me take the kids upstairs and put them in their cribs. McKenzie doesn't like them to be held long while they're sleep. She's trying to get them to sleep in their beds," Charmaine informed her.

"Sure, Tino and I need to be leaving to go pick up the kids soon anyway," Jennifer replied before getting up. She took my daughter from Tino's arms, and I handed my son to Char-maine. Once they were out of ear shot, Tino spoke up.

"Look, I know you don't want to hear this, but I'm going to say it anyway. I see the way you're looking at Kenzie, but don't even try to go there with her. I've been talking to her and she's not fucking with you like that. She's actually happy with Blaze and he seems like a cool dude. After everything you put her through, she deserves the chance to be happy. I'm not saying it'll work out between them, but you have to give her a chance to figure out what she wants without interfering."

I looked at my brother for a minute to see if he was serious. I couldn't believe he was going against the grain. He was basi-cally telling me to forget all about giving my twins a chance to have a two-parent home.

"Damn bro, I thought you were supposed to be on my side?"

"You know I am but at the same time, I look at McKenzie like a sister and at the end of the day, she's the mother of my niece and nephew. In order for her to be there and raise the kids properly, she needs to be happy and not stressed. You can't give McKenzie what she wants and needs. You keep saying you'll leave Diane alone for her, but even with you not being in a relationship with Diane you're still sleeping in the same house and bed with her. If you really wanted to end things with Diane, you would have done it already. McKenzie can never trust you that way, and you know it."

As bad as I didn't want to hear this shit, Tino was right. There was a part of me that can't leave Diane alone. To be honest, if I got into a relationship with McKenzie, I probably still wouldn't be able to leave Diane alone completely.

"You don't have to worry about that. I was just looking at her. She's already told me her mind is made up, and I'm doing my best to respect that for the sake of our kids."

"Have you talked to Ma today?" Tino asked, changing the subject.

I tried calling her earlier but she didn't answer."

"I talked to her this morning and she told me she had to work."

"Yeah, I bet she did," I replied sarcastically.

"Come on now, don't be like that. You know Ma is stubborn, but she'll come around eventually."

"At this point, it is what it is, Tino. I can't make her change her mind. I just hope she does it before it's too late."

My mother still hasn't seen my kids in person yet. She refuses to come out here or acknowledge them until I get a DNA test done and I'm not doing that, so right now we're not seeing eye to eye. I do call her to check on her and make sure she doesn't need anything because she's my mother, but that's about it. I can't push her to accept my kids and be in their life.

Tino and I continued our conversation until Jennifer came down the stairs. We said our goodbyes and they left the house, leaving me in the living room alone. I decided to go upstairs to the twins' room and sit in there with them. There is a sofa bed and a TV in the kids' room, so this is where I spend most of my time when I'm here, trying to stay out of McKenzie's way.

CHAPTER THIRTEEN
MCKENZIE

For the first time in a long time, I can truly say I know what happiness is. Everything in my life is going according to plan. Everything is in order from my goals down to my relationship. I started back taking my online classes and I just got hired part time as a customer service representative for FMLA. I know everyone wanted me to wait until the twins were at least a year old before I started working, but it's from home and I make my own hours. I want to work so I can save my own money. I don't want to depend solely on my father, brother, and Chase. I want to be able to say I bought something with my hard-earned money.

Now let's talk about my personal life. Things between Malakai and I are amazing. I couldn't have asked for a better man. It's like he was handpicked just for me. I experienced Malakai the friend, now I'm experiencing Malakai the man. He's loving and caring not only to me but to the twins as well. He doesn't have a problem checking in or showing affection. He stops by almost every night before he goes home, to spend time with me and the twins. Some nights he'll stay over just so he can listen out for the them while I get some sleep or studying done.

Being with Malakai is like coming down for a breath of fresh air. Everything I thought I knew about being in a relationship, he proved me wrong. I can't even compare him to Chase or Chris because neither of them is at his caliber. He's on an entirely different level of his own.

When I went for my six-week checkup, Malakai went with me and we both got tested for STDs. I've been tested before, but this was the first time that I actually got tested with a partner before we had sex. We also sat down and talked with the nurse about different birth control methods, and we both agreed that Nexanon would be best for me. With my busy schedule, I wouldn't remember to take my pills all the time and I didn't want to chance that. I love being a mother, but I have no intentions on being pregnant again no time soon. I meant what I said when I stated I'm not having any more kids until I'm married.

I stood in front of the mirror and stared at my naked body. I was amazed with the progress I've made over the past three months. When I got pregnant, I was one hundred forty pounds and by the time I delivered, I was one seventy. That was the largest I've ever been in my life. I didn't recognize myself when I looked in the mirror, and I lost my confidence along the away.

Malakai assured me that I didn't have to rush to get the weight off and he thought I was still beautiful no matter what, but I wasn't trying to hear that. I needed to feel it and see it for myself. Don't get me wrong now, I think thick women are beautiful. My sister, cousin, and some of my other family members are thick, but it just felt weird to me because I loved my pre pregnancy body.

I spent the first six weeks breastfeeding and counting calories. I lost most of the weight that way and when I was given the okay by my doctor at my checkup, I started working out to tone my body. I'm now one hundred fifty pounds. My bra cup went up a size and so did my jeans due to my thick thighs and ass. My ass still not huge, but it's plumper and more to grab on. It's to the point where I can't help but stop at every mirror I pass to admire myself. Some may call it conceited, but I call it confidence. I takes a lot to feel like this after giving birth to two kids, not to mention my hair is thicker and my edges.

Tonight will be the first time Malakai and I are going out as a couple. We've been taking our relationship at a steady pace and not rushing things. We haven't had sex yet, but that's all going to change tonight. We didn't discuss it, but we both know it's well overdue. I got my confidence and body back, now I'm ready to buss it open for a real nigga.

I spent the day getting myself pampered. I got my nails, feet, and hair done, then I went and I got my entire body waxed, including my vajayjay along with a vajacial. I put on my black lace panties with a matching lace bra that I just bought today at Victoria's Secret, before slipping on a black, fitted, long-sleeve mini dress. The dress stopped a couple inches under my ass and clung to my small waist. There was a deep plunging V at the neck that made my breasts look wonderful. I put on a black pair of red-bottom heels that made my legs look longer than they really are.

I touched up my makeup and ran my fingers through my hair. I squirted on my Versace Bright perfume and finished the look with my diamond necklace, chain, and bracelet. Malakai didn't tell me where we were going. All he said was for me to wear something that would make his dick hard, so I think this does the trick.

As I was grabbing my YSL clutch from the closet, there was a soft knock on the door.

"Come in," I called out.

I looked up and saw Tori standing in my doorway.

"Damn girl, you look good as hell. Try not to hurt him too bad tonight," she joked.

"Do you think it's too much?" I asked nervously.

"Girl no, it's just enough to turn him on but leave enough for the imagination. He won't be able to keep his eyes and hands off you tonight."

"Are you sure that you're fine with keeping the twins all night? I feel like a bad mother leaving them all night to go lay up with a man. We could just come back here after our date."

"Girl no, y'all waited a long time for this so it should be special. If you're here and you hear the twins crying, you're not going to be able to focus. Plus, you haven't had sex in months, so I'm not trying to hear your ass. Charmaine will be here with me, so we'll be fine."

"Thanks girl, I don't know what I'd do without you. Did you need something though?"

"Yeah, Malakai is downstairs and Chase is still in the nursery with the twins."

"Okay, I'm going to stop in there before I leave. Let Malakai know I'll be down in a couple minutes."

I put my phone, lipstick, wallet, and keys inside of my clutch. Those are the four most important things that I never leave home without. I turned my bedroom light off then stepped inside of the nursery to see the twins and Chase before leaving.

I walked down the stairs, and Malakai was standing by the island looking like he'd stepped out of a *GQ* magazine. He had on a black Dolce & Gabbana double-breasted suit with a white crisp dress shirt up under it and a pair of black DG dress shoes. I could see his diamond Patek shining from the stairs and the rock in his ear. The closer I got, his signature Bond No. 9

cologne filled my nostrils, causing me to clutch my things
together.

"Hey beautiful, these are for you," Malakai said as he
handed me a box of Venus ET Fleur royal blue roses.

"Hey, thank you, baby, these are gorgeous," I replied before
kissing him on the lips.

I sat my box of flowers on the counter, then we headed out
of the house. I turned on old school slow jams and set an inti-
mate mood during the drive. Malakai wouldn't tell me where
we were going still, so I just sat back and enjoyed the ride. I
stared out the window while Malakai went about ninety on the
expressway. From the direction he was going, it looked like we
were heading into the city.

After riding for almost thirty-five minutes, we were downtown. Malakai pulled up to the John Hancock building. He gave
the keys to the valet driver then we went inside of the building
and rode the elevator up to the ninety-fifth floor where The
Signature Room & Lounge was located. Malakai gave his name
to the hostess, then we were shown to our seats. It was one of
the most amazing views I've ever seen in my life.

As soon as we sat down, the waitress took our drink orders
and was right back to take our food order. We ate, drank, and
flirted during the entire dinner. Tori was right about Malakai
not being able to keep his hands and eyes off of me. He
couldn't keep his hands off my thighs, and I couldn't wait to
feel them all over the rest of my body.

Once dinner was over, we got the car and drove for about
five minutes until we made it to the magnificent mile. He
pulled up to Hilton Chicago and gave the valet his keys.
Malakai grabbed a bag from the trunk then we went inside of
the hotel. Malakai stopped at the front desk and gave his
name. He booked us an executive king room. The receptionist
attempted to flirt with him, but he ignored her and pulled me

closer to him. She got the hint and handed him the room key, then we went about our business.

We walked into the room, and it was beautiful. There was a trail of red roses from the door that led all the way to the bedroom with a heart made out of roses on the bed. There was a bottle of Moet on ice and chocolate-covered strawberries on a tray beside the bed.

I walked over to where the champagne was and poured us both half a glass while Malakai was pulling things from the bag he brought with him. He turned on his Beats pill and connected his phone to it. "Peaches and Cream" by 112 played while he turned the lights down, setting the mood.

Malakai took off his shoes and suit jacket before walking over to where I was.

"Let's propose a toast, to us," he said as he took one of the flutes from me.

"To us," I repeated before taking a gulp of the champagne.

Malakai sat on the edge of the bed and I immediately straddled him. I ran my hands through his thick waves before planting my lips on his. Every time I kissed this man, it was like he took my breath away. He kissed me with a sense of want and urge. I could feel his dick growing in his pants.

"Stand up and take your dress off," he demanded.

I stood from Malakai's lap and slowly pulled my dress off, allowing it to fall to the floor. I slowly wound my hips to the music that was playing on the loud speaker, making sure to keep eye contact with Malakai. His beautiful eyes turned dark as he licked his lips like he was ready to ravish me.

I sat down on Malakai's lap and gave him a lap dance. He unhooked my bra and caused it to fall to the floor with my dress. He massaged my breasts and roamed his hands all over my body. His touch was so gentle it felt like a feather was going across it. My entire body felt sensitive to his touch and he hadn't even done shit yet.

Malakai lifted me off of his lap and gently placed me on the bed. He stripped down to his boxers then hovered over me. He placed his lips onto mine and kissed me gently before sliding his tongue in my mouth. He broke the kiss and his lips went from my jaw to my neck and then further down my body, setting it on fire.

Malakai ripped my underwear off like it was a piece of paper before diving in head first. I grabbed the back of his head and rotated my hips to match his tongue movement. This man was a beast with his tongue. It slithered from my clit all the way to my ass, causing me to jump slightly. I started seeing stars when his tongue licked around my ass crack. I have never had a man eat my ass before.

"Oh my Goddd, Malakai, what the hell are you doing?" I panted as my body began to convulse. I started squirting like a broken faucet, and he stayed down there to catch every drop before latching back on with his tongue. He had me ready to tap out and I hadn't even gotten the dick yet. I lost count of how many times I came before he finally came up for air.

"You taste so fucking good, I can eat you for breakfast, lunch, and dinner," he said as he stood up and pulled his boxers off, releasing his thick, ten-and-a-half-inch dick. His dick was pretty as hell with a curve and a thick mushroom. I was salivating at the mouth just looking at it.

Malakai climbed back in the bed and placed his lips back on mine, allowing me to taste myself as he slid inside of me gently inch by inch, causing a moan to escape both of our lips.

I held onto his shoulders and dug my nails in them as gentle as possible as he stroked me slowly. He lifted one of my legs and put it over his shoulder, finally pushing the rest of his dick in until I could feel his balls slapping up against me. I couldn't tell whether I was coming or going. All of my senses were leaving and I could barely remember my name. This man's dick game was so good it should be illegal. I could tell why he said once we get together, I wouldn't want anyone else. I had sex plenty of times, but I have never been made love to, and that's exactly what Malakai was doing. He was capturing a piece of my mind, body, and soul with each stroke.

"Malakaiiiii, baby, I'm about to cum," I moaned.

"Hold it a little while longer. Can you do that for daddy?"

"Whatttt?" I cried out. I mean, like, I was literally in tears crying and pulling at my own hair. I probably looked like I was crazy as hell, but I didn't care. All I wanted to do was release the orgasm he built up and he was telling me to wait.

"You heard me, hold that shit. If you cum before I say so, I'm going to eat your pussy over and over but stop before you cum each time," he warned me, and he stroked me deep and slow, making sure to hit my spot with every thrust.

"Dadddyy, I need to cum," I cried out again as I clenched my pussy around his hard dick, causing him to stop moving for a minute. I had him right where I wanted him. If he wanted to play, I could play too. Those Kegel lessons were definitely being put to work.

"Fuck, baby, you can cum, ma," Malakai groaned as I continued to clench my muscles until I released my juices on his dick.

Malakai flipped me over and plunged into me from the back. He held onto my waist and beat my pussy up. He slapped me on the ass and pulled a handful of my hair. He reached between my legs and rubbed my clit, causing me to cum again. Before I knew what was happening, I felt him inch one of his fingers inside my ass. I couldn't explain how that shit made me feel. It was another first of the night.

Malakai and I alternated between fucking and making love

for almost an hour before we both were ready to tap out. I was too tired to get out of bed, so he went and got a towel then came back and cleaned my kitty. He turned the music off and threw the towel on the floor before climbing into bed with me.

"Are you okay? I didn't hurt you, did I? I was trying to be gentle, but your pussy good as hell and I haven't had sex since before we became official. I was trying my best not to bust after the first couple of strokes," Malakai said.

"I'm great, you were perfect," I assured him.

Malakai pulled me closer to him, and I placed my head on his chest and my threw my leg over his. We lay in a comfortable silence as I rubbed my fingers across his tattooed chest.

"I know this might be sudden to you, but I love you, McKenzie. I loved you before we even made this relationship official. You don't have to say anything back, I just couldn't hold that in any longer," Malakai confessed.

"I love you too, baby," I replied before closing my eyes. I had been wanting to tell Malakai that for a while, but I didn't want to feel like I was pressuring him or rushing our relationship.

It wasn't long after we confessed our love to each other before I was passed out with the biggest smile on my face.

CHAPTER FOURTEEN
BLAZE

The following morning, I woke up to one of the best feelings in the world. For a minute, I thought I was dreaming until I opened my eyes and saw McKenzie's head bob up and down as she sucked and slurped on my dick. She had her hand wrapped around it, stroking as she went up and down. She looked me directly in the eyes as she twirled her tongue around the tip of my dick, causing me to moan like a bitch. I tried my best to hold that shit in, but I couldn't.

"Fuck, ma, suck that dick just like that, baby," I groaned.

I leaned my head back to break eye contact because the way she was looking in my eyes while giving me head had me ready to bust already. It was one of the most beautiful sights I'd ever seen.

"Look at me or I'm going to stop," she threatened me. I couldn't believe she was using my own tactics.

I did as I was told because I didn't want this feeling to stop. I wanted to see if she was going to actually let me cum in her mouth or stop. If she let me cum in her mouth, she gone have my ass ready to go buy her a fat ass diamond when we leave this room.

McKenzie continued to stroked my dick before she took my balls into her mouth. She had my toes curling and eyes rolling in the back of my head. I thought Kim gave good head, but she ain't have shit on my baby. I see why Chase's ass risked it all with his woman for Kenzie after the first time they had sex. He was a dumb motherfucker for fucking up with Kenzie, because she's all mine now.

I grabbed the back of McKenzie's head and she picked up the pace, causing me to moan even louder.

"I'm about to bust," I warned her. When she didn't move, I shot my hot liquid down her throat. She made sure to catch every single drop of my nut. She continued to suck me dry. It felt like she was trying to suck my soul out of my dick. I guess this was payback for last night when I wouldn't stop eating her pussy. I couldn't take the shit anymore, so I pulled her pulled her up to me and kissed her, not caring that she had just swallowed my babies.

I sat up against the headboard and McKenzie eased down on my dick, causing a moan to escape both of our mouths. Her pussy was wet as hell just from sucking my dick. Shit like that made my dick even harder because that meant she enjoyed pleasing me just as much as I enjoyed pleasing her.

"Shit, Kaiii, this dick feels so good," McKenzie whimpered as she moved up and down on my dick. I held onto her neck and applied a little bit of pressure, and her crazy ass started smiling as her eyes rolled back and her mouth went in an O shape. She held onto my shoulders and picked up the pace. Her little freaky ass was enjoying every bit of this. I knew she was a freak the first time I laid eyes on her, and she had the nerve to act like she didn't want to give a nigga the time of day.

"Oh, fuck," I moaned as she turned around and did a split

on my dick. I grabbed a handful of her ass as she twerked on me. It was fatter than what it was when I first met her, and I was loving the view.

"Malakai, I'm cumming, baby," she called out before squirting all over my dick. That was another thing I loved about her. I didn't take much for me to make her cum and she was a squirter, so that meant her pussy was juicy as fuck.

I allowed McKenzie to catch her breath, then I climbed out of bed and pulled her to the edge of it. I threw both of her legs over my shoulder and plunged into her. I watched my dick as it went in and out of her. It was coated in her cum, and I only had a couple more strokes in me before I was ready to cum.

"I'm about to bust, baby. Where you want me to release this nut?" I boasted.

"Wherever you want, daddy," she purred.

"Open up," I ordered as I pulled out of her.

McKenzie sat up on her elbows and held her mouth wide open. I released my nut on her titties and in her mouth. She smiled at me as she rubbed my cum around her nipples. The site of it was making my dick hard again. I pulled up from the bed and went in the bathroom to finish what we started in the shower. I wouldn't have gone another round after we showered, but I was going to give her a break because at this point, she could barely stand.

"It's almost eleven, so we need to get ready and check out. I want to go to Wishbone to get something to eat before we head back to the house."

"Uhm, you tore up my underwear and I can't walk in those heels right now."

I chuckled as I walked over to the bag I brought in last night. I grabbed a panty and bra set from it along with a Versace jumpsuit and sneakers. I handed it to her, and she got dressed while I got dressed in a pair of black Amiri jeans and a long-sleeve, white, fitted shirt with a pair of black Versace sneakers.

Once we were both finished getting ready, we put our clothes and shoes from yesterday in a bag then we left the hotel and headed to breakfast. As soon as we got in the car to go home, McKenzie was out like a light. She was knocked out during the entire drive. When we made it to her house, I gently shook her awake.

I grabbed the bags from my car that contained some clothes and shoes I bought for the twins when I bought McKenzie's clothes. I know she's going to fuss about it because she keeps saying they don't need anything else, but as long as I'm buying stuff for me or McKenzie, I'll be buying things for them and my kids as well. We're all one big package deal together.

I took the bags upstairs to the kids' nursery where McKenzie was standing over Chance's crib rubbing her hair. I stayed at the house with them for about thirty minutes then left to go take care of some business at the warehouse.

When I went inside, all my men were working, just like I liked. We enjoyed playing hard, but we worked harder first. They were unloading products, packaging goods, and counting money. I spoke to everyone then went to my office.

I sat down and poured myself a double shot of Hennessey and rolled up a blunt. I'm not a chronic smoker. I only smoke maybe two blunts a day. I liked to sit back and wind down with it to ease my mind. I took the books from my drawer and went over the records for the past week. After I finished that, I got up from my desk and sat at my table so I could count the money I collected yesterday.

Two hours passed when there was a knock at my office door.

"Who is it?" I called out.

"It's me," Josh answered.

"Come in," I replied.

"What's up, man, how long you been here?" Josh asked.

"I made it here around two."

"You should've called me, I would have come in earlier."

"It's cool, you know I like to get this shit done early so I can chill in the evening."

"I know, but you and McKenzie's date was yesterday, so I thought you'd have a late start."

"Nah, I left her place around one thirty then came here."

"Cool, how was your night?" Josh questioned with a raised eyebrow.

I leaned back in my seat and smirked at his question. Josh and I don't talk about our sex lives on a regular, but there are occasions where the topic will come up if it's somebody new or something was wrong. It was something we could discuss in private and not have to worry about it getting out to anyone else. We don't go into full detail, but we do let each other know how it is. He and my brother are the only ones that can ask me that and actually get an answer. Anybody else would get cursed out because in my mind, that meant they wanted to fuck the girl I was fucking with.

"Man, let's just say it was worth the wait. She's a ten all the way across the board. Don't let her age fool you. She's giving these grown bitches a run for they money."

"Damn, even Kim?"

"Yeah, my shorty lethal. I already said she was going to be my future wife before we even took it there, now I know I would die a happy man being married to her," I laughed.

"That's what's up, man, I'm happy for you. It'll be good to have another married man in the crew to fight off temptation," Josh said.

Josh jumped in and helped me work until my phone started to ring. I looked down at it and saw that it was Tasia.

"Hello," I answered.

"Blaze, you have to come over now. Some niggas ran up in my crib looking for drugs and money. They were asking me where you lived and when I didn't tell them anything, one of them started beating my ass until I gave them the cash I had stashed. I told them I didn't have any drugs here, but they didn't believe me so they tore my shit up looking for it. Before they left, they pulled out a gun and threatened to kill me and Kayla," Tasia cried into the phone.

"Okay, try to calm down. I'll be there in a few minutes," I told her before hanging up the phone.

"What's wrong?" Josh inquired.

"I'll explain in the car, we have to go to Tasia's spot," I told him.

Josh and I rushed out of the warehouse and got in my car. I went damn near a hundred miles an hour on the expressway. I jumped back and forth between lanes as I explained to Josh what Tasia told me.

Seventeen minutes later, I was parking in front of Tasia's apartment. We got out of the car and walked up the stairs. Her front door was hanging off the hinges. I pushed it open and found Tasia sitting on the couch with her face in her palms. When she looked up, I could see the tears falling from her eyes. Her apartment looked like a tornado blew through it. Her TV was lying on the floor and all the furniture was cut up. The dining room table was flipped over. They even put holes in her wall. I told this damn girl she needed to move up out of here and her ass didn't listen, now she and my daughter were in danger.

"Oh my God, Blaze, I was so scared. I don't know what to do," Tasia cried as she approached me and wrapped her arms around me. I held her and rubbed her back to help her calm down.

Once she was calm, I lifted her head and examined her face. There was a light bruise forming under her right eye and a cut on her lip. I hated that this shit had happened to her.

"I'll take care of everything. Go hurry up pack some of you and Kayla's things so you can come home with me," I told her.

"How are you going to tell McKenzie that your baby mama lives with you now?" Josh asked once Tasia left the room.

"Man, I don't know. I'll explain what happened and hope that she trusts me enough to believe that nothing is going on between us. It'll only be for tonight though. Tomorrow I'm going to send them to Miami or Cali until I figure out what's going on. I just need to make some calls tonight."

"Okay, do you think I need to be trying to move my wife and kids?"

I was about to respond when my phone started to ring. I looked down at it and saw it was my brother.

"What's up, bro, I was just about to call you," I said into the phone.

"Hey man, I hate to have to do this, but you need to come meet me in Miami. Some shit went down and it's bad. I had to bring Myra and the kids out here. The jet will be there to pick you up in the morning at nine."

"Fuck, that's why I was about to call you. Some niggas ran up in Tasia's crib looking for me, and I have no idea who it was."

"This shit not a coincidence. You need to come now and bring her. We're staying at the safe house, so she'll have Myra and the kids to keep her company. Once they're settled in, though, we need to fly back to Cali to handle everything."

"Okay, text me the details," I said before hanging up the phone.

"What's wrong?" Josh asked.

"Some shit went down in Cali too. Mase is in Miami, I have to go fly out there in the morning and get them settled in, then we're going to Cali."

"Damn, I'm going to talk to talk to Nita and get some things in order then bring her and the kids out there in a couple days until the coast is clear. I'll come back out here and keep an eye on everything until you need me in Cali. Do you think McKenzie and Tamika will be good?"

"Yeah, nobody knows Tamika is my baby mama, and she lives in the burbs so she'll be good. McKenzie will be cool too. The security system on her house is on point and there's a panic room installed in her basement. Besides, nobody knows about her, and I plan on keeping it that way."

"You know it's not that simple, bro."

"I know, that's why I'm going to have to do something I know I'm going to regret."

"I'm sorry, I hope this shit don't take long so you can fix it."

All I could do was sigh because I hoped it didn't take long either.

We finished up at Tasia's house then I drove to the warehouse to drop Josh off before dropping Tasia off at my house. I helped her and Makayla get situated, then I left so I could go talk to McKenzie face to face. I dreaded the conversation I was about to have with her. I was about to go back on my word, and that shit was fucking with me. I was about to give Chase a chance to slide right back in her life and if he did, there was nothing I could do about it. I thought about it hard, and this was the only way that I could keep her safe. At the end of the day, I'll rather McKenzie hate me then get injured behind me and my street business.

CHAPTER FIFTEEN
MCKENZIE

I was in the process of pulling plates and cups from my cabinet when there was a knock on my front door. Tori was sitting on the couch watching TV, so she got up and answered it. I smiled when I saw Malakai walk in the house.

"Hey baby," I spoke.

"Hey ma, what you over there cooking?" Malakai asked as he walked over and kissed me.

"I actually just finished. I made fried chicken, baked macaroni, greens, and honey cornbread. Did you have dinner yet?"

"Nah, so make sure to take a plate out for me too," Malakai replied.

"Okay, I gotcha."

CJ started crying, so Malakai washed his hands then walked over and picked him up out of his rocker. It's crazy how I can tell my babies apart just from their cry. I even know what each cry means.

"What's going on, buddy, what you crying for? Do you need your diaper changed?" Malakai asked CJ as he rocked him back and forth.

"Is he wet? I'll come change him when I finish putting the food on the table."

"Finish what you doing. I can take him upstairs and change him," Malakai said. He walked up the stairs with CJ while I set the table and placed the food on it. I took three Sprites from the refrigerator and sat them on the table as well.

Typically, Tori would be helping me because we usually cook Sunday dinner together and all the other days, we take turns. However, today I was giving her a break for watching my kids all night. Tori agreeing to move in with me was a gift from heaven. When she's not at work she's here helping me out with the twins. I don't know who to thank more, her or Malakai. Without them, I'd probably be crazy or depressed by now. Taking care of two kids at the same time is no joke. Especially when both twins are hungry or crying at the same time.

Malakai walked back down the stairs and laid the baby in his rocker then joined us at the table. He kissed me on the side of my head, causing me to smile before he made his plate. I loved when Malakai came over and had dinner with me. He's here at least three days out of the week for dinner. He'd eat dinner then stay over and watch a movie afterward.

We all sat around and made small talk over dinner. Once we were done eating, Tori volunteered to clean up, so I took that as an opportunity to get the kids ready for bed. I took Chance from her rocker and Malakai picked up Chase. We went upstairs and Chase held both of the twins while I ran them bath water in their tubs. We washed their hair and bodies then dried them off. They were already falling asleep before we made it to their room. We put their diapers and sleepers on then put them in bed. I had already fed them right before Malakai showed up, so they should sleep until five. This was basically my routine, so I tried to stick by it because if they weren't in bed by nine, they would be cranky and keep me up all night.

I turned their projector on and stars danced around the ceiling while "Twinkle, Twinkle Little Star" played out loud. I turned the baby monitor on and turned the lights off then closed their door. I walked inside of my bedroom and found Malakai sitting on the edge of the bed. He looked like he had the world on his shoulders. I could tell something was off at dinner, but I didn't know what it was.

I closed my bedroom door and walked over to Malakai and straddled his lap. He looked up at me and smiled, but it didn't meet his eyes. I kissed his lips gently and his expression instantly softened as he kissed me back, but it wasn't like our typical kiss. He didn't deepen it like he normally did, and it didn't send tingles down my body.

"You look stressed right now, baby. Relax so I can help you relieve some of it. I need you to kiss me like you want to fuck me," I whispered as I kissed him on the neck then made my way back to his lips. This time he deepened it and kissed me the way that I liked it. He slid his hands up under my dress and made his way to the rim of my underwear. I stood up and stripped out of my clothes and Malakai did the same. Before I could react, he bent me over and ate my pussy from the back until I was cumming all over his face.

Malakai and I fucked on my bed, against the wall, and in the chair of my bedroom. Today was different than it was last night. Last night Malakai was gentle and held back some, but today it was like I was fucking Blaze. He was releasing the beast in him and not trying to hold back. It was like he was taking all of his problems out on my pussy, and I loved every bit of it too. Don't get me wrong now, I loved when Malakai made love to me, but I enjoyed that rough shit too. I liked to be manhandled, spanked, and choked during sex.

After fucking for hours, Malakai and I both collapsed on my bed. I laid my head on his chest and masked in the glory of our session. I reached up and rubbed Malakai's jaw line and he looked down at me and smiled.

"You're so fucking beautiful," Malakai said before leaning down and kissing me on the lips.

"Thanks, handsome, are you going to tell me what got you stressed? You're not like yourself and you were fine when you left me earlier."

Malakai sighed and looked up at the ceiling like he was battling what to tell me. He was starting to make me nervous because I've never seen him like this before. In all the time that I've known him, we have never not been able to talk about what was on our mind.

"McKenzie, you know I love you, right?" he asked.

I nodded my head, but that was strike number one in my book. Malakai starting a sentence off like that let me know he was about to say some shit I wasn't going to like. I've never heard anyone ask that question then finish it up with something good. If it was something good, he would have just told that he loved me and it wouldn't have come out as a question.

"Malakai, what the fuck is going on?" I asked as I sat up in bed, and he followed suit. Instead of answering me, he turned around and sat on the edge of the bed with his back facing me. That was strike number two because that was rude as hell. He had one more strike and I was swinging on his ass before he could give me a full explanation as to what was going on.

I climbed out of bed and walked around and stood in front of him with my arms crossed, waiting on him to explain what was going on. I wasn't about to be ignored in my own damn house. The suspense was killing me, though, because from the looks of it, whatever was going on with him was going to affect me as well.

Malakai finally looked up at me, and his eyes had a sense of sadness in them. Maybe something bad did happen and it didn't have anything to do with me. I was starting to feel bad for jumping to conclusions.

"Come on, baby, talk to me. Tell me what's going on," I practically begged. I wanted to try a different approach, then maybe he'd be more comfortable with telling me what's going on.

"Earlier today when I left here, I went to go take care of some business at the warehouse. While I was there, Tasia called and said some niggas ran up in her house looking for me. I went there to help her pack up some of their things because it's not safe, plus they tore her shit up. I planned on letting them stay at my house tonight, then I was going to send her and Kayla to Miami tomorrow. Before I left there, my brother called, and apparently some shit went down in Cali too, so he flew with his family out to Miami. I have to go meet him there to get Tasia settled in, then me and him are going to Cali."

I took a deep breath because I wanted all the facts before I jumped to conclusions. I didn't like that his baby mama was staying at his house, but I understood. He would be less of a man if he didn't protect his child. Tasia and I weren't cool, but I didn't want anything to happen to her. We kept it cordial for the sake of both of us being in Malakai's life, but I know that she still has feelings for him unlike Tamika, who's moved on with her life.

"Okay, so how long are you going to be gone for?"

"Honestly, I'm not sure. I'll be flying back and forth between here, Miami, and Cali trying to figure out what's going on and eliminating any threats. It could be for a month or so, I'm not really sure. I have to focus on finding out who's behind this shit."

"Alright, so where does that leave us?"

"You have to believe me when I say this is the last thing I want to do, but I think we should take a break. I don't know how long this is going to take and I won't be able to live with myself if you or the twins got caught in my crossfire. Niggas already ran up on Tasia and my brother in Cali. I have shit coming at me from left and right. I won't be able to focus on what I need to do and make sure that you're safe at the same time. As long as I'm out of the picture, you'll be safe because no one knows who you are yet," he said solemnly.

I took a deep breath and counted to ten in my head, trying to calm down. I had counted about two or three more strikes during Malakai's little explanation, and I was beyond pissed at this shit.

"So, let's get this shit straight. You finally get a chance to fuck me and now all of a sudden you're leaving town with your baby mama and we have to call it quits? Were you fucking Tasia still these past three months?"

"What? You know me better than that. I didn't stick around and spend time with you just for us to have sex, and I haven't touched Tasia since before me and you got together. None of what's going on has to do with me leaving you for her. If I wanted a relationship with her, I would have been had one with her. More than anything, I wanted our relationship to work. I really do love you, McKenzie. I'm just in a fucked-up position right now and me keeping you safe is the only thing I have control over," he explained.

"Fuck that, I'm not trying to hear that shit. You're being a fucking coward right now. You lied to me and said you loved me. You told me you were different and that I wouldn't have to worry about you hurting me. You fucking allowed me to get my feelings involved and fall for you," I yelled as I started punching Malakai in his chest. He stood there and allowed it until my fists started turning red, then he grabbed my wrists. My punches weren't affecting his muscular chest at all.

"Calm down, Kenzie, you're hurting yourself. You don't know how sorry I am for this. It was never my intention to hurt you in any way. I wish you could see that I'm doing this protect you. I'm a selfish man, but I can't be selfish when it comes to your life. If you don't believe anything I've ever said, believe me when I say that you are one of the most important people in my life. I can't sit around and ask you to pause your life for me because I have no idea how this will end. I can end up in jail or dead when it's all said and done, then I still wouldn't be able to come back home to you."

Shit, now why did he have to go and say something like that? I was still angry, but my heart softened some because what he said was true, but I wasn't going to let him off the hook that easily. If people were running up in his baby mama's crib and causing chaos in Cali, that meant shit was bad and he was going to have to get his hands dirty.

I snatched my wrists from Malakai and my chest heaved up and down. I could feel my eyes beginning to water, but my pride wouldn't allow the tears to fall. I refused to allow him to see me cry. I don't give a damn how much I cry behind closed doors, the days of me giving a man the satisfaction of showing them that they hurt me are over. This was the third relationship I had with a so-called friend that went to shit. Granted, he didn't cheat on me or was living a double life, but hurt is hurt.

"Don't tell me to calm down, I have every reason to be pissed off. Just get the fuck out, Malakai, go home to your baby mama." I said the last part to piss him off.

I know I'm being petty and probably immature too, but I don't give a fuck. He went back on his word, and it was going to take time for me to forgive that. I don't need his ass to protect me. I can do that on my own. I was trained on how to fight and shoot like all of the men that worked for my father and brother. I hated that Malakai saw me as some damn damsel in distress. I thought he knew by now that I wasn't some weak ass bitch that couldn't handle herself.

If he really wanted this relationship to work, he could have put in more effort. I'm a very understanding person, so I wouldn't be mad if I didn't see him all the time because he had business to take care of. Him not asking me to wait for him made it seem like he had plans on doing him while he's out in these streets taking care of business, and for that reason alone, I had no sympathy for this situation.

Malakai picked me up in one swift move and out of instinct, I wrapped my legs around his torso as he pushed me up against the wall.

"Stop fucking playing with me, McKenzie. I'm not leaving here with us on bad terms. I let you talk your shit because you were upset and have a right to be, but make no mistake, baby, I'm still the one in charge." He smirked.

"Your ass not in charge of shit over here."

"Really? Then why your pussy wet? I can feel it dripping on my stomach. You want me to take care of that for you, ma?"

I hated how my body betrayed me. I wanted to stay mad at Malakai but at the same time, I wanted to melt in his arms. I wanted him to hold me and never let me go. I shook my head no, but the word yes slipped out of my mouth, giving Malakai the okay to push me down on his rod. This time he led me back to the bed and made love to me like his life depended on it. When we were done, he held me in his arms and whispered how much he loved me over and over until I fell asleep in his arms for what might be the last time. At some point during the night, I felt Malakai release me and get out of bed. I couldn't bear to tell him goodbye, so I kept my eyes closed and willed myself back to sleep.

CHAPTER SIXTEEN
ANIYAH

Ever since Quan and I got married, my life has flipped upside down. It's only been three and half months, but it feels longer than that. I've been stressing the fuck out ever since. We went to Vegas and got married in the two-week span like we planned. The night we got engaged, we ate dinner then got on the computer to look up flights and hotels. Since our budget was tight, I found a twelve-hundred-dollar package for Vegas, which included our hotel stay for four days, three nights and round-trip flight. We flew through Spirit and stayed at The Strat Hotel. The hotel wasn't nothing to brag about, but as long as I was there with Quan I didn't mind.

We got married at Graceland Wedding Chapel by an Elvis impersonator and grabbed someone from a previous ceremony as a witness. At the time I felt thrilled about the situation. I was finally doing something for myself, not worrying about the consequences. The days we were there were pure bliss. We had no phones or contact with the outside world. We were in our own personal bubble, and that shit popped as soon as we landed back in Chicago.

Our honeymoon phase had come and gone. What should have been the happiest time of my life was straight bullshit. When we got back, we invited my parents over for dinner and told them we were married. I expected them to be happy for me, but they both seemed disappointed. My mother was more hurt than anything and my father was pissed. They couldn't fathom the fact that I got engaged and married without telling them. It was basically the same reaction with the rest of my family, so I started distancing myself from them.

I tried to make things right with Charmaine and she claimed to forgive me, but I'm not so sure. We aren't as close as we used to be anymore. She hated the fact that I got married to Quan. She had the same reaction as McKenzie. She called me all kinds of crazy bitches with no remorse for my feelings. I've only seen the twins twice in person since they've been born.

The first time I stayed for a couple hours, even though it was awkward because we didn't have much to talk about. I didn't know what to say and I still felt some type of way due to her reaction of me being with Quan. The second time was when she invited some friends and family over last month for a game night. After being there for an hour, I was ready to go home. Being there reminded me of all the things I was missing out in life.

The way Blaze was with McKenzie was sickening to me. They were acting all in love and shit. He looked at her like she was the only person in the room. I watched him cater to her every need. He helped her cook for the get together and cleaned. Seeing them was a reminder of what I was missing out on in my marriage.

I can count on one hand how many times Quan and I have had dinner together at home. The most time we spend together is when we're watching a movie, having sex, or sleeping. I thought things would be different now that we were married. Damnit, it's supposed to be different, but it wasn't. Our relationship was still the same as when we were boyfriend and girlfriend, only now we sleep in the same bed every night. Well, I don't even know if I can call it night because he doesn't get home until almost two in the morning every day. I guess I should be grateful that he doesn't allow the sun to beat him home.

Whenever I call him out on staying out all night, he uses the excuse that he needs to work harder to provide for me so we can start a family. I'm in school still, so he takes care of all the rent and bills. I try not to nag him too much because I feel that a man is supposed to be the provider, but I can't help but feel lonely. To make things worse, I don't have anyone I can talk to about this because I'm afraid to hear someone say I told you so.

I've been sick the past couple weeks, so I went and bought a pregnancy test. I was nervous about taking the test because I was afraid it would come back positive. I didn't want to tell Quan I was rethinking the decision of us having a baby. When the thought first came to mind, I thought it would be amazing to get married and start a family instantly with my husband. However, with the way things are going right now, I'm afraid that it'll feel like I'm a single mother, and I didn't sign up for that.

I went into the bathroom and peed on the stick. I sat it on the counter and washed my hands then played the waiting game. Five minutes passed, then I finally decided to look at the test. Just as I expected, the test was positive. I walked back in my room and sat on the bed. I didn't know whether to scream or cry. This whole situation was sad.

I got up and grabbed my phone then dialed Quan's number. I wanted to ask him if he could come home early so we can talk, but he didn't answer. I tried one more time and he still didn't answer the phone, so I decided to call McKenzie. She was the only person I was close to that had a baby and would know how I was feeling. I just hoped she wouldn't make me regret calling her, because I really needed my sister right now.

The phone rang three times before she finally picked up.

"Hey Niyah," she answered.

"Hey, can you talk right now?" I asked.

"Yeah, what's going on?"

"I took a pregnancy test and just found out I was pregnant. I'm scared as hell and don't know what to do."

"Why are you scared? What did Quan say?"

"He doesn't know yet. I just tried call him but he didn't answer. To be honest, things haven't been good between us lately. I don't know what's going on, but he says he's working late. I just don't know if I should believe him, not after what happened between him and Shavon."

McKenzie was silent for a minute. I'm assuming she was trying to think of what to say without hurting my feelings.

"You can say it, you can tell me that I made a mistake," I said when she still didn't say anything.

"Oh Niyah, I wasn't about to say that. I already told you what I thought about y'all getting married and then I left it alone. You're my sister and I love you, but it's your life to live. We all know what we can and can't tolerate in a relationship. I was just going to tell you that when you decided to marry him that also meant you were forgiving him."

"I know, Kenzie, I just don't know what to do. What can I do to get him to show me the attention I want and need? What is it that you do? I've seen the way Chris, Chase, and Blaze are with you. They all worshipped the ground you walk on."

McKenzie sighed before finally speaking.

"You can't compare yourself or your situation to mine,

Niyah. You love Quan and you two are married. You got him to stick around and put a ring on your finger, so you're doing something right. Men are just dumb asses for no reason. He's the only man you know and have ever been with. Chris, Chase, and Blaze might have looked like they worshipped the ground I walked on, but you have to look at the shit I had to deal with, with both Chris and Chase. I don't even have any words for Blaze right now. We broke up a couple days ago."

I was shocked to hear that. They seemed so happy together even before they were in a relationship. I wanted to know what happened but I didn't want to upset her, so I said the other thing that came to mind.

"I'm sorry to hear that. Are you okay? I know how you feel about him."

"It's fine, the situation was out of both of our hands. He had to go back to Cali to take care of some things and he doesn't know how long he'll be gone. I'm about to just focus on the kids, school, and work. I'm over men now."

McKenzie and I stayed talking on the phone an hour and a half before we hung up. We caught up on everything that had been going on with us. It felt like old times again and I loved it. I missed the tight bond we had and I know I'm to blame mostly for our strained relationship, but from now on I'm going to put my pride and jealousy to the side and be there for my sister.

I stayed up until almost two thirty before Quan finally decided to make his way in the house.

"Hey baby, what are you still doing woke?"

"I was waiting up for you because we need to talk. I've been calling you and you didn't answer."

"I'm sorry, my phone was in the back charging, and I was busy. I'm here now, so tell me what's going on," he said as he pulled me into his arms.

"I took a pregnancy test today and found out I was pregnant."

"That's what's up, it's what we wanted, right? Why you sitting here like it's the end of the world?"

"I don't know, Quan. Lately I've been feeling neglected and I don't want to have to be a single mother."

"Baby, you won't be a single mother. I promise I'll do better and be there for you and the kids. I just want to make sure that we don't have to struggle. I'm trying to stack my money so I can start a business. I'm not trying to be hustling all my life. I want to be able to be home with you and our future kids."

"Can you please just try to at least come home a couple nights out of the week for dinner? You don't have to stay in all day but just for a little while. I get lonely being here by myself all the time."

"Okay, I can do that for you, but I need you to do something for me. I need you to be patient with me and everything will fall in place for us. Can you do that for me, baby?"

"Of course," I replied.

Quan kissed me gently on the lips, then we went upstairs to our bedroom. We stripped out of our clothes and got in bed. Quan held me in his arms while we discussed what we could work on in our relationship. He was being attentive with me and I hoped it would stay like this. I guess only time would tell.

CHAPTER SEVENTEEN

MCKENZIE

Four months, one hundred twenty-eight days to be exact. That's how long it's been since Malakai left me alone in my bed. The first couple of weeks we stayed in contact with each other and talked every day, but that shit was hard for both of us. How could you talk to the person you love every day but know that you can't be with them? I cried myself to sleep every night after we hung up, so I told Malakai it was best that we slowed down on our conversations.

Malakai didn't want to agree with it, but he did. Our texts are limited to once a week, and we keep it simple. He texts to see how me and the kids are doing and I ask about him and Makayla. I know how Marquis is doing because Tamika's came over a few times and she brings him with her. I loved that little boy to death despite me and his father not being together anymore.

I'm still not sure how long Malakai is going to be gone. From what I heard, they found some of the people but they're still looking. Of course, I didn't hear that from Malakai because he doesn't want me knowing what's going on. I have Lauren to thank for that bit of information. She also told me that whenever he comes to Miami, he stays at the house with them and sleeps in my bed. I couldn't help but smile when she told me that because it meant I was living in his mind rent free just as much as he was in mine.

My birthday came around two months ago and Malakai made sure to call me and send gifts for me and the kids. I appreciated that, but it still wasn't enough. I've tried everything to get him out of my system and nothing works. It's like he's imprinted on my heart and mind. When I close my eyes, I can still remember the last night we were together. I can feel his lips against mine and his hands caressing my body.

I thought I was in love with Chris and Chase but now after being with Malakai, I'm not so sure anymore. I never felt the way I do about Malakai as I did with either of them. I don't know what the hell he did to me, but I don't like it. I hate feeling vulnerable and at this point, I feel like my heart is just a muscle in my body. I knew exactly what K. Michelle felt when she said she should have used her heart less.

I gave Malakai a chance and it didn't work out. Three strikes is all it takes for me to say I need to fall back and this love shit isn't for me. I've made myself numb to any feelings and pushed them all to the side. I'm more focused now than I've ever been. I'm getting straight A's in school and my job offered me a full-time position. Not to mention I got this motherhood shit on lock. I had to remind myself who the fuck I was and boss up. The only men I needed in my life were my father and brothers. However, my wants, that is an entirely different story. I'm twenty, sexy as hell, educated, and paid. I have my whole life ahead of me to settle down so for now, I'm just going to have fun and enjoy life.

Today was my monthly friends and family get together. It's something I've been doing every month since I had the twins. It's a way for me to stay connected with my siblings, cousins, and close friends. We play games, drink, eat, laugh, and fill each other in on what's going on with our lives. I look forward to this every month because this is the most time I spend with adults besides Tori. The weather is nice right now, so when I have free time I take the kids to the park or to the city to see my mother.

Everyone was out of my house by eleven as usual. We only spend four hours together then they all go their separate ways. Tonight was a little bit different though. Liam stayed behind to help me clean up, and I suggested he stay to have another drink with me. Since it's nice outside we decided to chill on my patio. I had a red and gray seven-piece patio rattan dining set. It came with three corner chairs, one table, and three ottomans

We went from drinking and talking to him nibbling on my neck and rubbing my fat ma through my boy shorts. The shit was feeling good as hell, and I needed more.

"Stop playing and taste it for me," I purred. I couldn't remember the last time Liam gave me head. He was one of those dudes that loved giving head more than he did fucking. Well, at least that's how he is with me. I can remember how many times we fucked as opposed to how many times he let me cum in his mouth.

Liam's fingers gripped the side of my boy shorts and pulled them down. He rubbed his nose across my pussy before dipping his tongue in. I held onto the back of his head and closed my eyes. I rotated my hips as he sucked harder. I was on the verge of cumming when I heard the sound of the house alarm beep.

My eyes flew open, and I pushed Liam out of the way. The

only people that were supposed to have keys to my house were my father, Martez, and Tori. My father and Martez were in Miami as far as I knew, and Tori was upstairs in bed. I hurriedly put my boy shorts and shirt on so I could see what was going on.

I rushed in the house and saw Chase standing by the door trying to figure out what my alarm code was.

"What the fuck are you doing in my house, Chase? Stop playing with my alarm before you have the police at my house," I yelled as I rushed over and put my code in. My brother had a fail-safe set up that if the alarm was put in wrong more than once the police will show up and we'll be locked in.

Chase ignored my questions and stared at Liam like he wanted to rip his head off his shoulders.

"McKenzie, tell your friend it's time to go. We have some things to discuss," Chase told me calmly.

Liam didn't even give me a chance to say anything. He grabbed his shoes and was ready to go just because Chase said so. This was one of the main reasons why I can never be in a relationship with Liam and he was stuck in the friendzone. His ass was scared of Chase, and everybody knew it. If we weren't such good friends, he wouldn't even have ever had the chance to see me naked. At this rate, he'll never see me that way again. He had just pissed me the hell off.

"See you, Kenzie, I'll call you tomorrow," Liam said before walking away. I didn't even bother responding to his ass. I just walked away because had he not grabbed his shit and left, I would have let him stay and made Chase get the fuck out. He was the one that showed up uninvited.

Since Chase was locking up behind Liam, I used that as cue to go upstairs to my bedroom. I was sexually frustrated and Chase's stalking ass had fucked my night up.

"I'm so fucking tired of this shit," I said out loud. Ever since Malakai had been out the picture, Chase thought it was okay for him to show up unannounced. He thought he was running shit and had a say in what went on in my life. I rummaged through my drawer and pulled out a nightgown to sleep in.

"What the fuck you tired of?" Chase asked as he stormed toward me.

"I'm tired of your ass. You always want to come over here and try to dictate some shit like you don't have your own house and a bitch there waiting for you."

"This is where my kids lay their head at night, so I do have a say in what the fuck goes on over here."

"Man, get the fuck out of here with that shit. You know your kids are good and well taken care of here. Now answer my question, how the hell did you get in my house?"

"I took your key one day when you were working and I snuck it back in," he confessed like the true stalker he was. I couldn't help but shake my head. I couldn't make this shit up if I wanted to.

"What are you doing here? You already came over and saw the twins earlier."

"I came to spend some time with you, but I see you had other plans. You back to fucking that nigga again? That's why the fuck you only got on that lil' ass shirt and underwear?"

I ignored Chase's question because he was on that good bullshit tonight. No matter what answer I gave him, we were going to end up tussling in this bitch. I guess he didn't appreciate me ignoring him because he yoked my ass up and pushed me up against the wall.

"Don't make me have to repeat my question, McKenzie," Chase seethed.

"No, I'm not fucking him, but he was in the process of eating my pussy when you showed up uninvited," I replied honestly. There was no use lying about it. I never lied about shit I do, and I wasn't about to start now. It wasn't like we were in a relationship anyway.

Chase grabbed me around my neck and applied just enough pressure to get my attention. As bad as I wanted to be mad at him, my kitty was thumping. His ass knew I loved to be manhandled.

"So, you were about to give that lame ass nigga some pussy? I know I told you and him that I better not find out y'all was fucking around. I accepted Blaze being around my kids, but I'm not about to have that lame ass nigga playing step-daddy to my kids too. You think he ready to get fucked up behind you?"

"I mean, you've been ready to risk it all for over three years. Can you blame him?" I smirked.

"Your lil' crazy ass think this shit a joke. You already know what I do to people that touch shit that belongs to me. If you don't want his family wearing all black, you better tell him you ain't fucking with him like that no more," Chase demanded.

"I'm starting think your dumb ass getting high off your own supply. I'm not an object and if I was, I still wouldn't belong to you. You got a whole bitch at home but stay worried about who I let between my legs."

"You are the mother of my kids so as long as I have breath in my body, you belong to me. I supply you with enough money and you can get the dick whenever you want to. You have no reason to entertain another man. Especially one that you're not in a relationship with."

"You're so fucking selfish, Chase. Who the fuck said that I want your dick? As far as I'm concerned, I'm free to do what-ever I want whenever I want. As long as your kids are not in harm's way, you have no say in what goes on here. My name is McKenzie, not Diane."

"How many times do I have to tell you that Diane and are not in a relationship? We just live in the same house together because you're playing games. All you have to do is tell me you want to get back together and I'll start back staying in my old house. You know I love the shit out of you. You're the one that I have kids with and the one that I want to be with. Let's not act like you ain't know I'm selfish when it comes to you."

I looked at Chase and wanted to cry, but I refused to shed tears in front of this stupid motherfucker. He actually thought what he was saying was alright. As if it was supposed to make me feel good about the situation.

"I'm tired of talking about this. Go home to your bitch," I said sarcastically.

"Nah, I'm where I want to be right now. I came over to spend time with you and our kids. I want to be able to wake up in the middle of the night to check on them for a change and wake up with you in my arms. If you need some dick, all you had to do was say something earlier when I was here. You know I'm only a phone call away."

"Those are a lot of damn wants, and if I wanted your dick you would have known earlier."

"Oh, so it's like that, you wanted a different dick tonight? The dick I been giving you the past couple months not good enough anymore?" Chase asked angrily.

I went two months without having sex after Malakai left. If I was horny, I used my vibrator and imagined it was him. By the time my birthday came around the vibrator wasn't doing the trick anymore, so I fucked Chase. I thought it would help me get Malakai off my mind, but the shit only worked about as long as the sex lasted. By the time we were done I was right back where I left off at, but that didn't stop me from letting him in every now and then. I know it's wrong, but call me selfish too. I got used to having someone in my bed at night.

"I'm not about to keep going back and forth with you about this. I just want to get in the shower then go to bed. You done sobered me right on up."

Chase looked at me for a minute before he released my neck. He leaned in and sniffed me before stepping back.

"You lucky I don't put my hands on females. Go take a shower and get his scent off of your ass now, then come get in the bed so we can watch a movie," Chase ordered.

I rolled my eyes but didn't say anything else before walking in the bathroom. I closed the door and turned on the shower. As soon as I got in, I released the tears I'd been holding.

I stood in the shower crying, trying to figure out how I was at this point in my life again. I hated that I still had feelings for Chase. I don't even know if I can call it love because I still loved Malakai. I wasn't even sure if it was possible to really love two people at the same time. I blame Malakai for this shit though. Had he still been in the picture, Chase would be a distant memory still. I mean, I was fucking happy, living the perfect life four months ago, and all of that changed in one day. It's crazy that all it takes is one day to fuck somebody's life up. Just thinking about it made me want to knock Malakai upside his head when I see him.

I finished my shower and dried off. I wrapped a towel around my body and walked into my room. I put on the night-gown I took out then climbed into bed with Chase. He had some movie playing on the TV, but I had no intentions of watching it. I turned my back to him and he had the nerve to wrap his arms around me and kiss the back of my neck.

"If you trying to bust a nut there's Vaseline under the sink in the bathroom. We're not fucking tonight, so you can back up," I said seriously.

I didn't give a fuck how horny I was. I wasn't about to

reward his ass with pussy after the stunt he pulled. That's like rewarding your child with a gift after they just got in trouble.

Chase sighed but didn't attempt to try anything with me because he knew I was for real. He just laid there and held me, which was fine with me.

CHAPTER EIGHTEEN

CHASE

It's been two days since I showed up at McKenzie's house with a key and she was still pissed off with me. I've spent both days trying to make it up to her. I tried to apologize, but she wasn't having it. I even stayed in all day both days and watched the kids while she worked and studied. I didn't know how McKenzie did this shit every day, because I was tired as hell. I felt like I should be giving her more money than I've been giving her for all the hard work she does. It made me feel like I wasn't doing enough when it came to helping with the kids physically.

I enjoyed being at the house with Kenzie and the kids. It felt like we were a mini family. I allowed McKenzie to sleep longer, and I was the one getting up at five in the morning feeding the kids and changing diapers while McKenzie got a couple extra hours of sleep. I made breakfast in the morning and McKenzie made dinner in the evening. We bathed and put the twins to bed together and watched TV before we went to sleep. The only thing missing from this scenario was sex. McKenzie was not letting me touch her even with us sleeping in the same bed together. I mean, I should be used to the shit because that's how it was with Diane most nights.

As much as I enjoyed relaxing in the house, I had to get back to work. I owe Tino big time because he's been taking on more of the workload for me since the twins were born. I try to make sure I spend at least three to four hours with them a day. I hate when I have to leave my kids, but I have no choice. I want to be able to keep them overnight, but McKenzie's not having it. She says I'm too busy and that I can't keep still long enough. In her mind, I won't do anything but leave them at the house with Diane.

I tried to convince her that wouldn't be the case, but she's not trying to hear that. If I lived on my own it would be a different story. McKenzie wouldn't have a problem with me keeping them alone. I'm not sure if McKenzie doesn't trust Diane or what it is. I know that no matter what's going on between me and Diane, she would never bring harm to my kids. She said she accepts them, and I believe her.

I looked down at my watch and saw that it was six o'clock. I need to find me something to eat. I haven't eaten since I left McKenzie's house around eleven. I've been busy as hell all day so food didn't cross my mind. I did drops earlier and pickups. I came back to the trap and counted money, now I'm sitting in my office with Tino going over the floor plan for the warehouse we bought last week. We're in the process of getting it gutted out and remodeled. This was something that was well overdue for us. We're looking to expand our business, so we need more room and a secure location to take care of business and have meetings.

I'm over this chilling in the trap stage. I have too much to live for and I'm not trying to get caught slipping in one of these traps because somebody turned on us. Besides, with the kind of money we're making, it's so much other shit we could be doing. It was time for us to step our game up. It should be finished in a couple months. The front half was going to be converted into a clothing store and the back would be where we kept all our products.

"How was your weekend with Kenzie and the twins?" Tino asked.

"It was good. I was mostly catching up on rest and spending time with the twins while Kenzie got a break. She was mad at me because I made a key to her house and threatened Liam's lame ass."

"Nigga, your ass crazy as hell. You lucky she ain't try to beat your ass for that shit," Tino laughed.

"Nah, she ain't swing on me. She cursed me out then went to sleep. She wouldn't let me touch her none while I was there."

"Damn, she must be really pissed off with you."

"Yeah, but I'm hoping that will change. Tomorrow I'm going to get the kids and watch them while McKenzie spends the day pampering herself with Tori."

"She letting you keep them on your own?"

"Not really, I told her that I was taking them to see Ma."

"Text me when you go over and I'll come help you with them."

A couple months ago, my mother finally came around and wanted me to bring the twins to see her. As soon as she laid eyes on them, she was attached. She still won't go to McKenzie's house, so I try to take them to see her twice a month. Once it gets cold out again, my ma is going to have to put her pride to the side and go to Kenzie's house to see them.

My mother apologized to McKenzie for everything that happened between them and Kenzie accepted, but neither of them wanted a relationship with each other. If they were in the same room together, they spoke or discussed the twins, but that was about it. My mother still felt some type of way about our situation, and she hates that I'm not officially back together with Diane, but she can't do anything about that.

I lit a blunt then Tino and I smoked while we waited on K.G. to bring the money from his drop. Everyone had brought their shit in except for his ass. I didn't know what was going on with him lately because he was barely showing up at the trap. After waiting another thirty minutes, K.G. came in with a Nike duffle bag.

"Damn nigga, took your ass long enough," I said.

"My bad, one of the guys on Cicero was short so I had to rough him up a bit," K.G. replied.

"How short are we talking?" Tino asked.

"A stack, I told him he had two days to come up with it or he was going to catch a bullet."

"Alright, where the hell have you been at lately?"

"Man, this bitch Nancy I used to fuck with showed up at my house a couple weeks ago with a little boy claiming it was mine. The shit was stressing me out because I never even knew she was pregnant. I got a DNA test done and the results came back positive, so I'm just trying to wrap my mind around everything."

"Damn, how old is he?" I asked.

"Three fucking years old. I choked the shit out of that bitch when the results showed I was the father. She made me miss three years from my child's life with no good reason for doing so."

"That's fucked up. If you need some time off just let us know so we can know what's going on. Disappearing and shit makes you look like you on some bullshit," Tino added.

"My bad, y'all my niggas though. Y'all are like brothers to me so I'll always keep it a buck with you."

K.G. handed me the bag then walked out of the room. Tino

had something to take care of at one of the other traps so he left me to count the money. I ran it through the machine and put a rubber band around each stack. It came out to $9,561. I wrote the amount in the books then put everything in my wall safe and locked it.

I was about to get ready to leave when there was a knock at my door.

"Come in," I called out.

Bri walked in my office, closing the door behind her. She walked over to me and straddled my lap. I slid my hand under her dress and gripped her bare ass cheeks. She was wearing a short sundress with a thong on.

"Hey baby, I missed you," Bri whispered in my ear.

"What's up, ma, you came over here to tell me you missed me?"

"No, I came over here to show you." She smirked before dropping to her knees.

Bri unzipped my pants, whipping my dick out. She spit on it then started massaging it to get it wet. She slowly licked me from the shaft to the head, causing me to bite my bottom lip. She put half of me in her mouth and used both hands while going to work.

"Fuck," I groaned as I fucked her mouth. She had slob and shit dripping down my dick. I pushed her head farther down until she started gagging and tears formed in her eyes. She sucked my dick for another five minutes before I pulled out of her mouth, beating my dick until I shot my nut all in her face, careful not to get it in her eyes. She licked her lips and got up from the floor. I grabbed the wipes from my drawer and handed her one so she could clean her face, and I grabbed one to clean my dick.

I stood up and fixed my clothes then reached in my wallet and handed Bri two hundred-dollar bills.

"Thanks baby, you know how to reach me if you need me," Bri said before walking out of my office. I was finished with everything I needed to do and I didn't feel like hanging out, so I locked up and left. I headed toward my house and stopped at Taco Bell before going in. When I entered, Shavon was laying on the couch scrolling through her phone.

"Well, look who the fuck finally decided to bring they ass home," Shavon spat.

"Mind your own motherfucking business and get the fuck off my dick," I yelled.

"Nigga, you wish I was on your dirty ass dick."

"Bitch please, I don't want that loose ass pussy."

"Yeah, aight, you better ask your boy about me," she replied.

"I don't have to. He's the one that told me you can suck a mean dick but that pussy trash." I smirked.

Shavon was about to respond when Diane walked into the living room with a bowl of popcorn.

"Hey D, I brought Taco Bell," I said, holding up the bag.

"Motherfucker, you been gone for two days, and you come scrolling in here like everything is fine. Where the fuck have you been?"

"I was at McKenzie's house." There was no need for me to lie about where I been. I didn't have anything to hide from Diane or anybody else.

"So you mean to tell me you been playing house with that bitch for two fucking days while I was worried about you? The least you could have done was answer my calls," Diane snapped.

"If something happened to me, my mother or Tino would have called and told you. McKenzie doesn't disrespect you or call you out of your name, so don't do it to her."

"Fuck that, I don't owe her respect. I gave her a pass the

first time because she didn't know about me. I actually felt sorry for her, but now is a different story. She knows we live together and she's still sleeping with you, so fuck you and that bitch," Diane snapped.

This wasn't even like Diane. She allowed Shavon's thot ass to get in her head.

"Fuck me? Who the fuck do you think you talking to, Diane?" I asked as I snatched her ass up by the front of her shirt.

"Let me go, Chase. What's wrong with you?"

"No, what the fuck is wrong with your ass? You better show me some respect and act like you know who takes care of all the bills in this bitch. We're not together, so I can do whatever the fuck I want to do. I could bring a bitch up in here if I wanted to, but I ain't on that shit. I was at Kenzie's house helping her with my kids. I'm a man before anything and I have to take care of my responsibilities."

"Your kids, that's all you keep fucking saying. You don't have to keep reminding me that you have kids. You don't have to keep throwing that shit in my face. Everybody knows you have kids with a bitch that's not me," Diane cried before walking away.

I looked at Shavon's nosey ass and she was sitting there shaking her head like a bobble head.

"I don't give a fuck about you shaking your head. I hope the motherfucker rolls off your shoulders," I shouted.

"Fuck you, dumb ass nigga. Kenzie gone use you to get what she want and then leave your ass again and when the time comes, I hope Diane don't be there for you again."

I ignored Shavon and left her sitting on the couch then walked into the kitchen. I sat at the counter and ate my food, thinking about what just happened. I still couldn't believe Diane had disrespected me like that. She's never talked to me like that in all the time that I've known her. I finished eating my food and threw my trash away.

I walked into my bedroom and Diane was laying under the covers. I could tell she wasn't sleep because I heard her sniffling. There wasn't anything I can say right now to make her feel better. I just needed to give her time to calm down because I still wanted to slap the shit out of her. I grabbed my stash of weed from the drawer then left out of the bedroom. I rolled me up a blunt before taking a quick shower.

Once I finished showering, I went into the guest bedroom and climbed in bed. I lit my blunt then called McKenzie on FaceTime to check on the twins. We talked for about fifteen minutes before hanging up. I grabbed my bottle of Patrón that was on the side of my bed and drank it from the bottle. Eventually, I started feeling buzzed and turned my lights off and fell asleep.

At some point during the night, I woke up to Diane bouncing up and down on my dick. The shit was feeling good as hell but at the same time, I was feeling dizzy. I was feeling the effects of the weed and alcohol. I tried to open my eyes but they were heavy as hell, so I squeezed them tighter. I was too tired to move, so I allowed her to do all the work until we both were cumming.

"For my pussy to be loose, it just made your ass nut in ten minutes."

I sobered up quick as hell and opened my eyes. The blinds on my window stay closed tight, so you can't tell when it's day or night in the room. I turned the light on and saw Shavon looking down at me smiling. I couldn't believe this bitch had just pulled this shit. I reached up and slapped her ass so hard she flew across the room.

I jumped out of the bed and lifted her ass up from the floor by her throat.

"What the fuck is wrong with you? What would make you do some dumb shit like this?" I seethed.

"I wanted to see what that dick do that got my cousin being a damn fool. I can see why she won't leave your ass. I wouldn't mind sharing you either. Your dick better than your boy's too." She smiled. I couldn't believe she had the nerve to smile.

"Get the fuck out of my house right now and I won't mention this to your cousin," I said.

"Nigga please, she won't believe you. All I have to do is tell her you came on to me and with the track record you have, she'll believe me. I'm not going any damn where but to the living room, unless you want to go another round." She smirked.

I opened my bedroom door and threw Shavon out of it, making sure to lock it this time. I climbed back in the bed and lit me another blunt. I needed to calm my nerves because I was ready to go out there and put a bullet in her head. This was something McKenzie or Diane could never find out about.

I knew Shavon was a trifling ho when she started fucking Quan. She was doing it to hurt Niyah, but this time she did something to hurt her own cousin. Diane has done nothing but be there for her. If she found out about this, it will crush her. I felt like shit, and this wasn't even my fault. I would never touch Shavon, even if I wasn't with McKenzie or Diane. I'm not attracted to the bitch and I hate her guts. She better be out of my house when I get up later or I'm going to beat her ass. I was so pissed I couldn't even fall back to sleep. I laid there for what felt like hours before I finally nodded back off.

CHAPTER NINETEEN

DIANE

Two weeks passed since Chase and I got into that argument. We were barely on speaking terms, and he was still coming and going as he pleased. Can't nobody tell me that he and McKenzie not fucking still. Those kids are only seven months and they don't need that much damn attention. I'm sitting around crying and bitching over his ass though. He's reminded me one too many times that we're not in a relationship anymore. It's funny how he only brings that up when he's angry with me. He doesn't mind acting like we're in one when he wants food, sex, or his clothes washed.

I'm doing all that shit for him. He's already getting sex from McKenzie, so she might as well feed and wash for his ass too. I'm tired of Chase and everything that comes along with him. I still love him, but I can't stand his lying ass. I'm too young and fine to be sitting around like I'm some bum ass bitch with nothing going for herself.

I made friends with some of my coworkers at the bank. They've been trying to get me to go out with them ever since I started working there last year, but I always decline. I've never really been into clubbing. I can actually count how many times I've been to one. Chase goes to them all the time, but he never takes me. He claims that's not a place for a woman in a relationship to go, and I listened. I was at the prime of my life sitting around like a lame. The days of not doing things because Chase says so are over. It's time for me to enjoy myself and not care what he thinks. Since he hasn't been home all day again, I'm going to the club and not telling him. It's not like he tells me where he's going.

I looked myself in the mirror and smiled at how good I looked. I had on a light coat of makeup and my 24-inch sew-in was bone straight. I was dressed in a short black skirt and a red off-the-shoulder shirt with a pair of red wedges. Just as I was squirting on my perfume, Kelsey text and said she and Justin were outside.

I grabbed my purse then headed out of the house. Kelsey got out of the front seat and got in the back. I knew she did that because Justin has a thing for me. We exchanged numbers a while back and he's a cool guy. He's dark skin, a couple inches taller than me with a slender build and handsome face. He doesn't look as good as Chase, but looks aren't everything.

Kelsey played on her phone while Justin and I talked about how our day was. I actually talk to him more than I do Chase, and that says a lot since Chase and I live together. We pulled up to the club thirty minutes later and Justin gave the valet driver the keys. The line to the club was long as hell and I was already regretting coming. I was walking toward the line when Kelsey stopped me.

"Girl, we not getting in that long ass line, our name is on the VIP list," she said.

"Thank God," I sighed, causing Kelsey and Justin to laugh.

Kelsey gave our names then we walked inside of the club.

The club was already packed and it was only eleven. Partygoers were drinking and dancing to the music. We walked through the crowd until we made it to a booth in the back where a couple more of our coworkers were. We all spoke then sat down.

Someone had already ordered bottles of Patrón, Hennessey, and Cîroc. I wasn't much of a drinker, but I was going to drink and enjoy myself tonight. I knocked back a couple shots of Cîroc and was feeling it already. I stood up from my seat and pulled Kelsey up with me and started dancing. I had a nice size ass and knew how to work it. She kept hitting me on the ass as I twerked. After a while, I felt someone walk up behind me. I turned around and saw that it was Justin then smiled. He held onto my waist as I danced on him to some mix that was playing.

I closed my eyes and gyrated my hips, trying my best to keep up with his beat. I had never danced with a man like this before, but I was enjoying the feel of Justin's body against mine. When I felt his manhood growing, I decided to take a break.

Justin and I sat back down with the group and had more drinks. I was glad I decided to come out with them. This was some of the best fun I've had in a long ass time. If I knew going to the club was like this, I would have been going. It's like I've been living under a rock and missing out on life. I can't ever remember laughing and smiling this hard in my life.

Kelsey stood up to go to the bathroom and pulled me by my arm to go with her. We stood in the line for almost ten minutes before we made it inside of the bathroom. I expected her to use it, but all she did was look in the mirror and fix her hair. I couldn't believe we stood in line all this time just for this, so I made myself pee since we were here.

"So, it looks like you and Justin are having fun," Kelsey said.

"Yeah, he's actually cool. I'm glad I came out with you all."

"I'm glad too. I hope this isn't the last time."

"It's not, I'll definitely be doing this again." I smiled.

I'm not saying I'll go clubbing on the regular, but I do plan on doing it every now and then.

I washed my hands then we walked out of the bathroom. We were almost to our section when I felt somebody grab my arm. I was ready to go off until I turned around and saw that it was Chase.

"What the hell are you doing here?" he asked.

"I'm here with some friends of mine," I replied.

"Why didn't you tell me you were coming?"

"Had you brought your ass home this week, maybe I would have thought about telling you but you didn't, so I didn't feel the need to call and tell you. You didn't tell me you were coming here either," I said.

"I didn't tell you because I'm here working. Some shit is about to go down, so whoever you here with, you need to let them know so y'all can get out of here."

"I'm not going anywhere. I don't say shit about you going out and I don't give you a curfew so you can't give me one," I snapped.

Chase looked at Kelsey then pulled me closer to him.

"Shut the fuck up sometimes. I'm telling you to leave for y'all safety," Chase said, looking around the club.

I sighed and snatched away from Chase and walked toward our section. I told everyone what Chase said, and they stood up to get their things so we could go. My feet were hurting so I held onto Justin's arm to keep my balance.

We were almost out the door when Chase snatched me off of Justin's arm.

"You can go get the car then I'll be right there," I told Justin. Justin looked from me to Chase then back at me hesitantly. I gave him a slight smile to reassure him that it was okay, then he finally walked away.

"What the fuck is this shit, Diane? You out here with some other nigga in public embarrassing me in front of my people."

"How the fuck am I embarrassing you, Chase? The last time I checked, you said we weren't in a relationship. If you're able to fuck your baby mama and any other bitch, then I should be allowed to do me. I don't give a fuck about your people. They're the same people that smile in my face knowing you lay up with another bitch damn near every night, so miss me with that shit," I snapped.

The liquid courage was really kicking in. I was finally saying everything that's been on my mind all this time.

"You know what, I'll let you have this one, only because I'm here dirty, but I can guarantee you this conversation isn't over. You better not have that nigga in my house or your ass going to end up homeless," he warned me.

I rolled my eyes at Chase and walked away. I was feeling good and buzzed. I wasn't about to allow Chase to ruin my mood.

By the time I made it outside, Justin was sitting in the car waiting on me.

"Where's Kelsey?"

"She's going to her man's house so she's riding with Andrea since she lives by him," Justin replied.

"Awe okay," I simply said.

The car ride from the club was fairly quiet and damn near awkward. I think it had more to do with me making it that way.

"Are you okay?" Justin finally asked.

"Yeah, my ex just pissed me off," I stated, shocking myself. That was the first time I've ever addressed Chase as my ex, even though that's probably how he mentions me all the time now.

"Do you want to go somewhere and talk about it?"

"We can go somewhere, but I don't want to talk. I just want to forget the conversation with him ever happened."

Justin nodded his head up and down as he drove. About twenty-five minutes later, we pulled up in front of Justin's condo. He helped me out of the car and we went inside. I was glad that he didn't take me home because I knew Chase might actually come home, and I wasn't in the mood to argue with him. I wanted to be able to enjoy my buzz.

When we made it inside of Justin's house, I took my shoes off then sat on his couch. His placed looked like the typical bachelor pad. Kind of how Chase's looked before I moved in and added pictures and colors. Justin walked in the kitchen and a few minutes later, he came back in with a bottle of wine and glasses. He poured me a glass then sat down next to me. I was nervous as hell and it felt like I was going to jump out of my skin. I had never felt this kind of attraction with another man besides Chase.

Justin and I were halfway through the bottle of wine when shit started to heat up. He had my body on fire when his lips brushed up against my skin. I tried to control my breathing so I wouldn't embarrass myself. I didn't know what it was, but Justin didn't touch me like Chase does. He was showing me more passion as well as taking his time. He was being attentive to me and I was enjoying the feeling.

I thought I would feel bad about what I was doing, but I didn't. As much as Chase cheated on me, I never thought about being with another man until now. I felt like I would be violating, but I didn't care about that anymore. I'm sure a lot of this has to do with the alcohol, but they always say alcohol doesn't do anything but remove your inhibitions.

After what led to a heated make-out session, Justin and I ended up having sex right there on his couch. His manhood wasn't as big as Chase's was, but it did the job and it made me cum a couple times. To be honest, I was able to take his dick better than I could Chase's. That's why when we made it to his bedroom, I had no problem going another round.

CHAPTER TWENTY
BLAZE

The past five months without having McKenzie in my life have been hell. I went from seeing her every day to not being able to see her at all. Ending things with her will always be my biggest regret. I miss them so much it fucking hurts. I don't feel like myself anymore because I left part of my heart and soul in Naperville with McKenzie. I'm man enough to admit that I'm incomplete without her and I won't be complete again until she's in my arms. I've turned all my emotions off and not allowed myself to feel anything but anger and hatred toward the niggas that fucked with my family.

When I made it to Miami to meet up with Mase, I found out that someone had burned down two of our trap houses with a large amount of our shipments in them. There was also a rat in our crew that was close to my brother. We didn't have to worry about him anymore, though, because I rocked his ass to sleep. You could call me the Grim Reaper, because I've been sending niggas to meet their makers.

With my personal life being in shambles, I've had more

time to focus on this shit street and I'm knee deep in it right now. I've been flying between Miami, Cali, and Chicago dropping whoever may be involved and taking what they stole from me. Every time I come back to Chicago, I'm tempted to go see McKenzie. I've been keeping up with how she's doing through Nita and Tamika. I'm glad I could count on Josh to hold shit down in Chicago when it comes to my legal businesses. Once I make it back, I'm treating him and his family to an all-expense paid vacation to wherever they want to go.

After planting spies and bugs, we found who was responsible for everything. It's taking longer than I expected, but we had to be smart about the situation. We took out all the small people that were involved and we got most of our products back and theirs. Tonight, all of this shit was finally coming to an end. We were ready to take out the big fish. We've been working on this plan for four months and I prayed it went as planned. If it did, I was hopping on the first flight in the morning to go back to Chicago and get my girl back. I don't give a fuck if she's been fucking with anyone else; she is still mine and I plan on fighting for her.

I'm willing to look past anything that she's done while I was away. It was my fault and I brought it all on myself. I hate to even think about her allowing another man in her bed, but it's not like I've been practicing celibacy either. The first couple of months I had sex with Tasia whenever I flew to Miami to see Makayla. I had to end that shit, though, because Tasia started acting clingy and expressed how she wanted a relationship with me. That was something I could never give her. If I did that, it would make it seem like everything McKenzie said was true, and it would make me out to be a liar. I assured Kenzie that I wasn't leaving her for Tasia, and I could never break her heart that way. I love Tasia because she's the mother of my child, but I'm not in love with her. McKenzie was and still is the love of my life.

I tried explaining that to Tasia, but she wasn't trying to hear it so I stopped staying at the house with her and started sleeping at McKenzie's family house. I could have slept in one of the guest bedrooms, but I wanted to sleep in my baby's bedroom. It smelled just like her, so in a way, it felt like I was close to her.

I looked down at my watch and saw I had a couple hours left before it was time for us to leave. I passed the blunt I was smoking to Mase and picked up my Glock. We were chilling and mentally preparing ourselves for the mission. We needed to make sure that all of the pieces were good. None of us could afford for the shit to jam.

"You good, baby bro?" Mase asked as he passed the blunt back to me.

"Yeah, I'm just trying to clear my head before we go out there."

"I know you miss your girl, but I need you focused. Going out there and getting yourself killed won't do anything for her or your kids. Not to mention it would crush the family and Ma would kill me. I miss my wife and kids as well, so I'm ready to end this shit just as much as you. I think you should call McKenzie before we go out there today. I know y'all haven't been talking on the phone, but hearing her voice might help calm your nerves. Plus, this shit we about to handle is major and we don't know the outcome. She deserves to know how you feel about her still. It's just something for you to think about. I'm about to go call my wife, so I'll see you in a bit," Mase told me before walking away.

I sat back and thought about what my brother said, and he was right. I needed to talk to McKenzie because there was no guarantee I would make it out alive tonight. I had men scoping the location out and the men there had heavy security. You might be wondering why we won't just give up, but that's not an option. I've given up more than I was willing to already. My brother and I bust our asses to get where we were and keep our father's legacy going, only for a jealous nigga to come around and try to take it all from us.

We found out that Elijah, one of our father's old business partners, was behind this shit. Apparently, he felt some kind of way about our father handing everything down to us. He figured we'd fuck up and destroy our father's business so he could scoop in and take over. However, we did the exact opposite. We were bringing in way more money than our father ever did, and Elijah couldn't handle it so he started scheming behind our backs and making deals with new people. My mole said he's been planning this shit for years. He was waiting until we were at the top to try and knock us down. If that happened, he would be in charge of everything and the new supplier.

I got up from the couch and went upstairs to my bedroom. I opened the door and sighed when I saw Kim laying in my bed naked.

"Kim, get the fuck up out of my bed and put some clothes on," I demanded.

"Are you sure you want me to put clothes on?" she asked as she approached me.

"Yes, I don't have time for this shit. You should be ready to do your part in this mission and not be trying to fuck me. If you fuck this up, I will kill your ass," I threatened her.

"You don't have to worry about that, baby. I'm ready, I just wanted to come help you relieve some of your stress before you go out there. I don't know what I would do if anything happened to you."

"I'm good on that, Kim. I have a phone call to make in private, so get out and go get ready."

"Okay, if you change your mind, you know where my room is." She smiled. Kim picked up her robe and put it back on then walked out of my room. I closed and locked the door then sat down on my bed.

Kim was the other person I've been sleeping with while I was away. I tried not to slip back to my old habits, but I was a man with needs. I didn't want to go around sleeping with random women I met in the streets, and I definitely wasn't going to start anything with anyone else because all of this was just temporary. I knew what I was getting myself into with Kim, and I didn't have to sell her false dreams.

I'm out here in these streets stressed, and I need a way to release the pent-up energy. Since Kim is around, I figured I might as well use it to my advantage. Don't get me wrong now, I know how to be faithful and keep my dick in my pants when I'm in a relationship. I never touched Kim or any other woman while McKenzie and I were official. I was faithful the entire three months that McKenzie made me wait before we slept together.

I had even cut off contact with Kim during the time I was with Kenzie. Josh reached out to her on my behalf if we needed her to take care of business for us. I would have cut her off completely, but she was one of my best workers. I had paid good money for her training to become a master manipulator and seductress.

I hadn't seen Kim in almost eight months before I sent for her to come out here. I called her because we needed a pretty face and nice ass to get close to Elijah's henchman. He liked slutty, submissive women, so that's what we transformed Kim into. We gave her a brand-new identity and he fell for her. All it took was for her to fuck him a couple times before he started pillow talking and giving out all of their plans. She had the man thinking he was in love. Her pussy was powerful to a weak nigga, and that's exactly what he was. You had to be weak nigga to give out all your boss's plans to a bitch you barely knew just because she had good pussy. I actually kind of felt bad for the sucker. Once she was in good with the henchman, she made her move on Elijah.

I wiped my palms on the front of my pants before calling McKenzie via Facetime. Talking to her wasn't enough. I wanted to see her face as well.

I was nervous as hell about calling her. What if she hated me and didn't answer? What if she was laid up with some nigga right now? All of those thoughts left my mind when I her beautiful face popped up on the screen.

"Helllooo, Malakai, are you going to say something?" she sang into the phone with her angelic voice. I smiled hearing her say my name because she refused to call me Blaze. She and my mother were the only people that called me Malakai to this day.

"Hey, McKenzie, I'm here. How are you and the kids doing?"

"We're doing good, they're getting so big now," McKenzie said as she flipped the camera on her phone and showed me the twins. They were both sitting up in their play pen playing with toys. She had sent me pictures of them a couple months ago, but they were way bigger now.

"I can't wait until I can see them in person again. I ordered some things for them, and it should be there in couple days," I told her. Even though I wasn't with McKenzie anymore, I still made sure to send stuff for both her and the kids. She told me that I didn't have to, but I wanted to. I owed her that much because I promised I would be there for them no matter what. That's why they were added to my will. If anything ever happened to me, they would be getting something the same way Tasia, Tamika, and my kids would.

"Thank you, how are you doing though?"

"I'm good, ma, I just really needed to hear your voice. I miss you so fucking much, Kenzie. I hope you can bring yourself to forgive me when all of this is over," I said.

"Is everything alright, Malakai?"

Ouch, she didn't tell me that she missed me. I hate to admit it, but that hurt.

"Everything's fine, I just needed to hear your beautiful voice and let you know I missed you. I regret ending things with us, but I still think it was the best thing to do to keep you safe. All of this will be over soon, and I'll spend the rest of my life making this up to you. I still love you just as much as I did when I left."

McKenzie got me sitting here feeling like a bitch right now. I've never had a problem with confessing my feelings. It's the rejection part I have a problem with, but I needed to let her know all of this while I had a chance.

McKenzie was silent for a minute and put me on pause. I thought she was about to hang up until I heard her sniffling. She was tugging on a nigga's heart strings right now. She had me ready to say fuck this mission but if I did that, then this would all be for nothing.

"I'm sorry, McKenzie, I didn't mean to make you cry. I understand if you don't feel the same way. You don't even have to say it back. I just needed a reason to smile for a minute. I have some business I need to go take care of, so I'll talk to you later." I was about to hang up until McKenzie unpaused the screen.

"Malakai... I love you too," she said before hanging up the phone. All it took was seeing her face and I felt a hundred times better. I got up from the bed and took a quick shower. I was ready now more than ever to get this over with since I knew it was a chance it would be a happy reunion between Kenzie and me.

The guys and I went over the plan one more time than we were out of the house and headed to Elijah's warehouse. We were going to murk everyone in there and take their supply. We were rolling in twenty deep. We got dropped off a block away and headed to the warehouse on foot. We had ten minutes to take care of everyone, then our drivers would come to the front to pick us up and the products.

We all put our ski masks on our faces and ran up in the warehouse. Guns were blazing everywhere. It was like a scene from a gangster movie. Some of our men were getting hit and so were theirs. That was the casualty of war. I made my way to the back where I knew Elijah's office was. I kicked in the door and the fat motherfucker was so engrossed in Kim sucking his dick that he didn't see me coming.

"That's enough, baby, I'll take it from here. Unless you want that fat nigga's cum in your mouth, then I'll wait." I shrugged.

"Thank God, the shit couldn't even stay hard. You owe me double for this shit," she replied.

"Don't worry, you'll be compensated well," I told her.

"Alright, I guess I'll leave you gentlemen to it then," she stated before walking out.

"Come on, son, we can work something out. You don't have to do this. I have kids and grandkids."

"Fuck your kids and grandkids. You didn't think about my family when you had niggas running up in my baby mama's crib," I bellowed.

"I was never going to hurt any of them. I did it to send a warning," he stuttered.

"Well, here's my response to your warning, fat mother-fucker." I lifted my nine and sent a bullet to his head. I let another one off for good measure before walking out of the office.

I went to find my other men and there were bodies all over the place. My men that weren't injured were helping the injured ones up and taking them out of the building. The rest of them were loading the product and money into a truck. We had hit the motherfucking jackpot and all this shit was over. I could finally go back to Chicago and build the life I want with McKenzie. Unfortunately, that thought was short lived when I felt bullets riddling my body. I'm guessing one of Elijah's men must have been hiding somewhere while everything was going down.

I could hear my brother yelling my name and someone returning fire as my body hit the ground. My life flashed before my eyes, and the last picture in the frame of my thoughts was McKenzie's smiling face. If I had to die, at least I can die a happy man knowing the woman I'm in love with loves me too.

To be continued...

ALSO BY KEVINA HOPKINS

Made in the USA
Las Vegas, NV
16 January 2024

84479266R00104